# Little Miss Stoneybrook...and Dawn

**Look for these and other books
in the Baby-sitters Club series:**

# Little Miss Stoneybrook...and Dawn

## Ann M. Martin

AN
**APPLE**
PAPERBACK

SCHOLASTIC INC.
New York Toronto London Auckland Sydney

Cover art by Hodges Soileau

ISBN 0-590-43717-8

12 11 10 9 8 7 6 5 4                                          1 2 3/9

Printed in the U.S.A.                         28

*This book is for*
*David Charles Eichhorn*
*With lots of love*

# CHAPTER 1

"Order! Order, please. Order!" Kristy Thomas rapped on Claudia Kishi's desk with the eraser end of a pencil. "This meeting of the Baby-sitters Club will now come to order — and I mean it!"

Kristy was having trouble getting our attention. The members of the Baby-sitters Club were kind of wound up. We were getting two new official members that afternoon, Mallory Pike and Jessi Ramsey, and besides, we'd had a half-day off from school because of teachers' meetings.

Mary Anne Spier, Claudia, Jessi, Mal, and I (Dawn Schafer) were all sprawled around Claudia's room, talking and laughing. Kristy was looking down on us from the director's chair she always sits in, and she didn't seem too happy.

Before I go any further, maybe I should explain who the club members are, and what

1

the Baby-sitters Club is. I'll start with the club, which was Kristy's idea. She and Mary Anne used to do a lot of baby-sitting in their neighborhood, and Kristy realized that any time a parent needed a sitter, he or she had to make about a zillion phone calls trying to find someone who was free. She thought, Wouldn't it be great if a parent could make one call and reach a whole bunch of sitters at once? So she got a group of friends together to form the club, and now we meet three times a week — Monday, Wednesday, and Friday afternoons from 5:30 until 6:00. Our clients know about our meetings (we advertise), and they call us while we're holding them. There are six members of the club now, and usually at least one of us is free and can take any job that comes in. Great for the parent (only one call to make, plus we are responsible, trustworthy sitters). And great for us (we each get lots of jobs, have fun, and earn money).

We run our club very professionally. We sitters are always on time, we make sure we know important information, such as where the parents will be and when the children should go to bed, and we're just plain great with kids. We love them! We have a club record book in which Mary Anne keeps track of our clients and appointments (she's the secretary), and I keep track of the money we earn (I'm the treasurer). We also have a club notebook, which is like a diary. (Kristy makes us keep it up to date.) In it, we each write up every job we go on, and then we're supposed to read the entries about once a week. That way, we know what's going on with the kids the other club members have taken care of.

And we have club officers. Kristy is the president, of course, since she thought up the club. She's outgoing and, well, okay, she's a little loud. As she says, her mouth gets her in trouble sometimes. When Kristy first started the club she lived right across the street from Claudia and next door to Mary Anne. She and Mary Anne had been best friends all their lives. Then last summer Kristy's mom, who had been divorced, married Watson Brewer, a really rich guy. Watson moved Kristy and her family across town to his mansion. Kristy has three brothers — Charlie, who's seventeen; Sam, who's fifteen; and David Michael, who's just seven. Now she also has a stepsister and stepbrother. They're Watson's kids. Karen is six and Andrew is four. Kristy likes her new family, but it represents a big change for her and she has a lot to get used to. Luckily, Charlie drives her to and from club meetings (we pay him out of the dues money we put in our treasury each week), so Kristy doesn't have to miss out on anything just because she moved.

Claudia is our vice-president. This is mostly because she's the only one of us with her own personal phone and a private number, so her room is the best place to hold our meetings. Claudia is as different from Kristy as it's possible for two people to be. Claud and Kristy are both thirteen (so are Mary Anne and I), but Claudia is a hundred times more sophisticated. Kristy couldn't care less about clothes; Claudia is a fashion nut who is always wearing the latest fad thing and looks great. She's Japanese-American and has this long, silky, jet-black hair; dark, almond-shaped eyes; and a creamy, clear complexion. She loves art and reading mysteries, but she's not a very good student. Which is too bad because her older sister Janine is a genius. Claudia and Janine live with their parents and Mimi, their grandmother, who is the best grandmother you can imagine.

Our secretary, as I've mentioned, is Mary Anne. She and Kristy are pretty different, too — opposites, almost — but they're best friends anyway. Kristy is loud, Mary Anne is quiet and shy. She's also sensitive (prone to crying) and a good listener. Kristy thinks boys were put on this planet to torture her, Mary Anne is the only one of us with a steady boyfriend. (Her boyfriend, by the way, is Logan Bruno, one of our club's associate members. That means that Logan is someone we can call on if a job comes in that none of us is free to take. Our other associate member is a girl named Shannon Kilbourne, who lives across the street from Kristy.) Although Mary Anne didn't used to care about clothes, lately she's been taking more of an interest in them and she's been looking good. One thing about the two best friends that's the same is their appearance. They're both small for their age and have brown hair and brown eyes. Mary Anne lives with her dad and her kitten, Tigger. (Her mom died a long time ago.)

Then there's me. I'm the new club treasurer. We used to have another treasurer, Stacey McGill, who was one of the original members of the club, but she moved to New York City, which was really sad. We all miss Stacey, Claudia especially. Claudia and Stacey were best friends. Anyway, when Stacey left, I became the new treasurer. I was not an original member of the club. That's because I moved to Stoneybrook, Connecticut, just last January. Less than a year ago. Until then, I'd lived in California with my parents and my younger

5

brother Jeff. But then Mom and Dad got divorced, so Mom moved Jeff and me all the way across country to this little town, which is where she grew up. I like Stoneybrook, but I'm a California girl at heart. I like hot weather, not cold, and health food, not junk. And I dress with style, but it's my own style. I'm very independent. Maybe you're wondering what I look like. Well, I have long, long (waist-length) pale blonde hair and blue eyes. I get freckles if I stay out in the sun too long. And here's something else you should know. Our house in Stoneybrook is over two hundred years old and has a *secret passage*. That's the truth.

Okay. Our new members are Mallory and Jessi. They're younger than the rest of us — eleven years old — and for that reason they are junior officers. (They haven't even been made official club members. That will happen today.) Mallory is the oldest of eight kids, so she knows a lot about handling children. She has dark curly hair, wears glasses, and is getting braces. She desperately wants pierced ears, but her mother says no. She and Jessi (Jessica) are alike in a lot of ways, except that Jessi is black. Jessi also wears glasses (just for reading) and thinks her parents treat her like a kid. (She's not allowed to have her ears pierced yet, either.) Like me, Jessi is new to Stoneybrook. She and her parents, her eight-year-old sister Becca (short for Rebecca), and her baby brother Squirt (nickname for John Philip Ramsey, Jr.) have only lived in Stoneybrook for a few weeks. Jessi is a super-talented ballet dancer. (She has these incredibly long legs and a thin, graceful body.) She and Mallory both like horses and reading.

Now you know about us club members, so let's get back to the meeting.

After a lot of pencil-rapping and ahem-ing, Kristy finally got our attention and we quieted down.

Kristy sat up very straight in the director's chair. She adjusted her visor. "As you know," she said, "today we are going to induct two new members into the club."

Jessi and Mal grinned at each other, but I thought, *Induct?* Who's Kristy kidding? First she comes up with this fancy word which just means to introduce them into the club officially. Furthermore, she didn't induct *me* when *I* joined the club. She just nodded to Mary Anne, and Mary Anne asked me if I wanted to be a member. Later, we did say a toast over pizza, but there was no actual *induction*. Exactly what did Kristy have in mind? I could guess. A speech and fanfare. Kristy likes to make a big deal out of things. Why hadn't she made a big deal when I joined the club? Because she was jealous of me, that's why. She was jealous that Mary Anne and I got to be good friends almost as soon as I moved to Stoneybrook. Kristy was used to being Mary Anne's only good friend. Well, she's gotten over that jealousy, I think, but she never bothered to *induct* me, so I minded (just a little) that she was going all out for our new members today.

Before she could get started, though, the phone rang.

"I'll get it!" Claudia, Kristy, Mary Anne, and I shrieked.

Kristy was closest to the phone, so she reached it first. "Hello, Baby-sitters Club," she said. "Hi, Dr. Johanssen. . . . Yes, she's here. Hold on." Kristy handed the phone to Claudia. "She wants to speak to *you*," she said.

The rest of us frowned. That's not how our club operates. Whoever answers the phone is supposed to find out the details of the job, hang up, offer the job to all of us, and then call the client back to say which one of us will be sitting. Often, only one of us is free since we're pretty busy, so there isn't any fighting over who gets the jobs.

And our clients know this. So why was Dr. Johanssen asking to speak to Claudia?

8

We found out soon enough.

When Claudia hung up the phone, she said to Mary Anne, "Put me down for Tuesday, three-thirty until six."

"*Why?*" Kristy demanded to know. She paused, then said vehemently, "Claudia, you can't do that!"

"How come?" asked Mallory.

"How come? Because the Baby-sitters Club doesn't work that way, that's how come," I exploded.

Mal blushed. She looked at Jessi in embarrassment. "Sorry. I didn't know," she said.

"Oh, Mal, I didn't mean to yell at you," I told her. "It's just that this is practically our most important club rule. And Claudia just broke it." I looked at Claudia. "Why?" I asked.

Claudia sighed. "Dr. Johanssen said Charlotte especially asked for me to be her sitter." (Charlotte is the Johanssens' eight-year-old daughter.) "She said Charlotte really misses Stacey and she knows I'm Stacey's best friend. This isn't my fault. I guess Charlotte just feels connected to me." Claudia shrugged and looked uncomfortable.

This *never* happened. I wished Charlotte had asked for me. It made me feel like I wasn't a good sitter or something, even though I knew that wasn't really true.

9

"Well," said Kristy huffily, "if that's what Charlotte wants." Kristy must have felt the way I did.

"I guess she does," agreed Claudia, still looking uncomfortable.

"I mean, it's not as if the rest of us haven't done some pretty great baby-sitting stuff," Kristy went on. "*I* was the one who thought up the Kid-Kits Charlotte likes so much." (Kid-Kits are boxes that we fill with toys and games, puzzles and books, and sometimes bring with us on sitting jobs.)

"I was the one who got Jenny Prezzioso to the hospital that time she got sick," said Mary Anne.

"I once saved two kids from a fire when I was sitting in California," I pointed out.

"Oh, you're all good sitters," Claudia jumped in. "Really." (Then how come I didn't feel like one?) "Char just misses Stacey, that's all. This is a special job."

Kristy tried to start up her induction ceremony again then, but the phone kept ringing. We lined up three jobs — for me, for Kristy, and for Mal and Jessi together at Mallory's house. (The Pikes always require two sitters because of all those kids.)

"See that?" said Claudia. "What are you guys worried about? You're great sitters. You're getting jobs. Forget about Charlotte."

We did. At least long enough for Kristy to cram in her induction ceremony before the meeting ended.

The ceremony went like this:

Kristy slid out of the director's chair. She picked up the club notebook and held it in front of her. Then she asked Mallory to stand on her left and Jessi on her right.

"Now," she said, "face me, and put your right hands on the notebook."

Jessi and Mal did as they were told.

(I looked at Claudia and we rolled our eyes.)

"Repeat after me," Kristy continued. "I promise to be a good, reliable, and safe sitter, and to be true to the Baby-sitters Club forevermore."

Mal and Jessi repeated this oath (which I'm sure Kristy had made up on the spur of the moment).

"I now pronounce you junior officers in the Baby-sitters Club," said Kristy.

Mary Anne burst into tears. "Oh, that is so beautiful!" she said.

Claudia and I rolled our eyes again.

"Well, six o'clock," announced Kristy. "Time to go home."

The meeting ended.

Later, I wished it never had.

# CHAPTER 2

I really love our house. It's the one thing about Connecticut that's better than California, at least in *my* mind. Our house in California was very nice, but there wasn't anything special about it. It was ten years old, built on one level, ranch-style, and looked like every other house on the street. I used to think that if it weren't for our bright yellow front door, I wouldn't have been able to tell it from the other houses. I might easily have walked into the wrong house after school one day and found a family that wasn't mine at all.

But our house in Connecticut is wonderful and special. As I've said, it's over two hundred years old. It's a colonial farmhouse with a secret passage that was probably once part of the Underground Railroad, which helped slaves escape from the South during the Civil War. Because the house is so old, the doorways are low, the stairs are narrow, the rooms are small and dark. Mom and I love it.

Jeff hated it.

To be fair, I should say that my brother hated most things about Connecticut. I'm not thrilled with things myself, but I learned to adjust. Jeff didn't. He tried to at first, I think. But after awhile he stopped trying. And he became impossible to live with. When he wasn't sullen and silent, he was yelling at Mom and me, or being rude. He got into one scrape after another in school, too. His teacher was always calling my poor mom or arranging conferences with her.

In fact, the evening after Kristy's little induction ceremony started out like a lot of other nights — with yet another phone call from Jeff's teacher.

Mom and Jeff and I were just finishing our dinner. We were eating brown rice and a vegetable casserole. I'll never understand how the people on this coast can eat so much red meat and white rice and disgusting stuff. Our family is into health foods.

It was a typical meal. Jeff didn't utter a word, except to point out rudely that my mother had gotten a big ink stain on her blouse. I should mention that our mom is totally absent-minded.

I always have to check her over before she leaves for work. If I don't, she's apt to walk out the door wearing two different shoes, or with only one of her eyes made up. I don't mind this. It's just part of who Mom is, but Jeff had been giving her a hard time about it.

Anyway, I don't know how Mom had gotten the ink stain, but I wasn't surprised that she'd forgotten to try to scrub it off. I *was* surprised that Jeff was so rude about it. I'd noticed the stain, too, but I was going to mention it later, when we were cleaning up after dinner.

Jeff didn't wait, though.

"Mo-*om!*" he exclaimed as soon as he sat down at the table.

"What?" replied Mom a bit sharply. Jeff was getting on her nerves.

"Look at your blouse. That is so gross."

I kicked Jeff under the table.

He kicked me back.

Mom looked at her blouse. "Oh, *no!*" she cried. "*Darn*, when did that happen?"

"Everyone at the office was probably laughing at you," Jeff muttered.

"Jeff, that was uncalled for," said Mom.

"Sorry," Jeff replied, not sounding the least bit sorry.

We ate a pretty silent dinner.

14

Just as we were starting to clear the table, the phone rang.

Mom answered it. "Oh, hello, Ms. Besser," she said, after a pause.

Jeff groaned. Ms. Besser was his teacher. Her call could only mean he was in trouble again.

"What'd you do this time?" I asked him as he and I continued to clear the table.

"Fight," he replied. "I got into a fight."

"And?" I prompted him.

"Well, it was Jerry Haney's fault. He started it."

"But what'd you do to him?"

"Gave him a black eye."

"Oh, good going, Jeff," I said. "You'll be lucky if you aren't expelled. I'm surprised Jerry isn't blind yet." (That wasn't the first black eye my brother had given Jerry Haney.)

When Mom got off the phone, she looked sternly at my brother. Then she pointed to one of the kitchen chairs. "Sit," she ordered.

Jeff sat.

I kept on cleaning up, hoping that if I did I wouldn't be asked to leave the room. I wanted to stick around for the fireworks.

My plan worked.

But there were no fireworks. To my surprise,

Jeff began talking before my mother did. And he sounded calm and rational for once. He took a deep breath. Then he bit his lip.

"Mom," he finally began, "I'm sorry about what happened at school today. Really I am. I couldn't help it. It's like, all I can think about is California and Dad. And I get really mad that I'm not there with him. There's this sort of anger bubbling up inside me all the time. And then when something happens, like Jerry making his stupid-jerk comment today, all that anger boils over. Do you know what I mean?"

"I think so," said Mom quietly.

"Do you think I need to go to a psychiatrist or something?" asked Jeff worriedly.

"Well, Ms. Besser certainly seems to. That's what she was calling about."

Jeff nodded. "What do you think, Mom?"

"I think I want to know what *you* think."

Jeff widened his eyes. He was used to getting yelled at, not asked his opinion. "I think . . . I think that if I could move back home — I mean, to California — all those anger bubbles would go away."

"Like somebody turning off the fire underneath you?" I asked.

"Yes!" Jeff said gratefully. "Like that. Couldn't I try it, Mom?" he went on. "Just for six months. If things aren't better after that, then

16

I'll come back here. I promise. But things *will* be better," he added.

I looked at Mom, horror-stricken. Surely she wouldn't let Jeff go.

"Mom — " I began.

"Not now, honey," she replied. She turned to Jeff. "This is the most difficult thing I've ever had to say," she told him, and her voice began to shake, "but I think you're right. I'm not sure what to do about it — after all, I have legal custody of you. However, I do think you've made some good points and should be allowed to try living with your father. I'll make a few phone calls." I could tell that Mom didn't feel nearly as sure of herself as she sounded. She must have been hurting — a lot — inside.

At that, Jeff's eyes gleamed with excitement, but he kept his cool. He didn't go leaping and prancing around the house. He didn't even say, "I told you so." He just sat in the chair while Mom began making phone calls.

I sat next to him. I was so mad I wanted to strangle him. I knew he needed to get out of Connecticut, but couldn't he see what he was doing to our family? It was bad enough that Mom and Dad were divorced. Still, Mom and Jeff and I managed to seem like a little family. If Jeff left, it would be hard to think of Mom and me as a family. I love my mom, but I knew that the two of us were going to feel like the ends of a loaf of bread, with all the other slices gone. I wanted at least one more slice. And Mom was going to let it go.

My mother talked on the phone for over an hour. She called her lawyer. She called her parents (my grandparents, who live here in Stoneybrook). Then, when it was late enough, she called Dad. (California time is three hours earlier than Connecticut time, so she had to wait until it was at least 9:30 here, to be sure he had come home from work.)

Most of the conversations sounded the same. Mom would explain the situation and her thoughts. Then she'd begin saying, "Mm-hmm," and "Yes?" and "Oh, I see."

I couldn't really tell what was going on and had to wait until after Mom hung up with Dad to find out. Then she turned to Jeff and me, who were still sitting right where we'd been for an hour.

"Well," said my mother, "we're working on it, Jeff. The lawyer thinks she can make it happen, since we're all in agreement that this is the right decision."

"All *right!*" exclaimed Jeff. "Thanks, Mom!"

"You little twerp!" I said to him hotly. "You are a rotten, spoiled baby."

"Dawn!" cried my mother.

I ignored her. "Can't you see what you're doing?" I yelled at Jeff. "You're breaking up what's left of our family."

"No, I'm not," Jeff replied quietly. "I'm giving Dad some of his family back. It's time we evened things up. Besides, I have to try this or I might end up in jail."

Mom and Jeff and I all began to laugh. The laughing felt good, but it didn't take away my hurt. Even if Jeff was a twerp, he was my brother and I would miss him. I already missed my father. Now I'd miss Jeff, too. And Jeff would have Dad all to himself. The lucky stiff.

Jeff got up to go to his room. When he was gone, I glanced at Mom. I knew there were tears in my eyes. They were about to overflow. Mom's eyes looked just the same as mine.

"Honey," she said, "you may not believe this, but Jeff is going to miss us as much as we'll miss him. And as much as we miss your father."

I shook my head. "I don't think so," I said, and suddenly all those tears started to fall.

Mom held out her arms to me. "Come here," she said.

And as if I were four years old again, I crept around the table and right into Mom's lap. We hugged each other and cried.

After we were done, I went upstairs. I sat

down on my mother's bed, still sniffling and gasping and sighing. When I thought I had my voice under control, I called Mary Anne.

I needed to talk to someone. I needed someone my own age to say to me, "It'll be okay. Honest. Call me anytime. We can always talk."

Which is exactly what Mary Anne did say, because she's the perfect friend.

(And I should add that Mom is — almost — the perfect mother.)

# CHAPTER 3

*D*ing-dong.

I rang Claudia Kishi's bell fifteen minutes before the beginning of the next meeting of the Baby-sitters Club. Mimi, her grandmother, answered the door.

"Hi, Mimi!" I said. (We all just love Mimi.)

"Hi, Dawn. How are you?" Mimi answered carefully as she let me inside. (Mimi had a stroke last summer and it affected her speech. She talks very slowly now and sometimes forgets words or mixes them up. But she's much better than she used to be.)

"I'm fine," I replied. "How are you?"

"Good . . . good. How about a cup of tea before the meet?"

"Oh, no thanks." It was a very nice offer, but all I wanted was to go to Claud's room and veg out. I hoped the meeting would be a quiet one. I was still feeling rotten about Jeff.

"Okay. I see you." Mimi waved me upstairs.

I grinned at her, then ran to Claudia's room.

"Hey, you're early!" Claudia greeted me.

"I know. I felt like hanging out for awhile."

"Great."

Claudia was lying on the floor, reading the latest edition of the *Stoneybrook News*. Ordinarily, she does not enjoy reading, but we all like the local paper. We especially like this feature called "Crimewatch," where they list all the robberies and other bad stuff that's happened in town. It's really fascinating. Claudia told me that around Halloween last year, forty-two pumpkin-smashings were reported.

"What's in 'Crimewatch' today?" I asked Claud, settling down on the floor beside her.

"Not much," she replied. Only it sounded like she said, "Mot mush," since her mouth was full of licorice. Claudia is a junk-food nut, and she's got stuff stashed everywhere — stuff I wouldn't touch with a ten-foot pole.

"What, though?" I wanted to know.

"Well, let's see. A man on Dodds Lane reported a burglar in his yard, but when the police arrived, they couldn't find anyone. And . . . on Birch Street a woman said she was being attacked by giant butterflies demanding Twinkies."

"Where?" I shrieked. "Where does it say that?"

"Just making it up," Claud replied, grinning. "Really. It was a light week, crimewise."

Claudia flipped back to the beginning of the paper.

"Hey, what's that?" I said. I pointed to an article on the first page. It was titled "Little Miss Stoneybrook Pageant."

Claudia looked where I was pointing, and we read the article together. A pageant to choose Little Miss Stoneybrook was going to be held for girls ages five to eight. The winner would go on to a county pageant. The winner of the county pageant could compete for the Little Miss Connecticut crown. From there, she could go on to try for Little Miss America and then Little Miss World. The Little Miss World crown seemed like kind of a long shot to me.

Claudia began reading aloud. " 'The contestants will be judged on poise, talent, and looks,' " she said. " 'The title "Little Miss Stoneybrook" does not signify merely beauty, but brains and talent as well.' " Claud dropped the paper and made a face.

"What?" I said.

"I don't know. I think pageants are sexist. I don't care what the article says. People go to pageants and they think that the only thing little girls are good at is dressing up and looking cute. That's . . . that's . . . it's like . . . what's

23

that word that sounds like tape deck? Stereo-something."

"Oh, stereotyping," I supplied. I felt myself blushing. "I know what you mean, but guess what. When I was two, Mom entered my picture in a baby contest in Los Angeles and I won."

"You're kidding! Your mother doesn't seem like *that* kind of mother to me. You know, the pushy stage-mother mother."

"Well, she isn't. She wasn't," I replied. "I think someone dared her to enter me. So she did and then I won. She was really embarrassed. Not because I won," I added quickly, "but because my picture appeared everywhere, so all Mom's friends found out what she'd done — and they didn't all believe it was a joke."

Claudia giggled.

"Anyway," I went on, "you should hear her stories about the mothers and kids who enter those contests. Some of them are really serious. Winning contests is, like, their career."

Kristy and Mary Anne showed up then and we read the article to them.

"Sexist," said Kristy. "Who'd want to do a dumb thing like be in a pageant?"

"A little girl might," spoke up Mary Anne. She accepted a piece of licorice from Claudia.

24

"I can see how it might be glamorous to be up on stage in a fancy dress."

"True," agreed Kristy. "I guess a pageant could be sexist . . . but fun."

Mallory and Jessie held a different opinion, though. They arrived at 5:30 on the dot and looked at the newspaper article.

"On, no! I don't believe it!" Mallory cried. "A pageant here in Stoneybrook. What a disgrace!"

"Yeah," agreed Jessi. "Pageants are *so sexist*. Do you ever see *boys* competing for a crown? For Little Mr. America or something? No," she answered herself. "You do not. At least, not very often."

"I can only hope," said Mal, "that my sisters don't hear about the pageant. Claire and Margo would want to enter for sure."

"Would that *really* be so bad?" I asked. "I mean, I guess a pageant *is* sexist, but . . . I don't know . . ."

"But it could be fun," Kristy finished for me.

I didn't thank her. I was still a little mad about the induction ceremony she'd made up for Jessi and Mal, but not for me.

"Well," Jessi said, "one thing I don't have to worry about is *my* sister entering the pageant. There's no way she'd do that. She has

25

terrible stage fright. Last year, when she was in second grade, her class put on *Little Red Riding Hood* in the school auditorium. Becca played a flower. Halfway through the play there was this big crash. Becca had fainted — right onstage."

We all laughed.

"Okay," said Kristy. "Time to begin the meeting." She paused. Then, "Claud?" she said sweetly. "How did your *special* job with Charlotte Johanssen go?"

"Oh, fine," replied Claudia. "It really wasn't such a big deal that Dr. Johanssen wanted me instead of any of you guys." She was looking uncomfortable again.

It was no wonder. We were all giving her the evil eye.

And I suddenly felt this incredible urge to prove to everybody, especially our new junior members, that I was as good a baby-sitter as Claudia was, if not the best sitter in the club.

The other girls must have been feeling the same way, because just as I was about to tell about saving the kids from the fire, Mary Anne said loudly, "I really *did* have to get Jenny Prezzioso to the hospital in an ambulance. It was quite frightening. But I kept my cool."

If Mary Anne weren't being such a good friend to me these days, I think I would have said something like, "*I* was *with* you, remember?"

As it was, Kristy said, "We have *all* heard about that particular emergency more than enough."

(I saw Mal and Jessi exchange a worried look.)

*Whew.* It was a good thing I hadn't mentioned the fire again.

Then Kristy added, "And by the way, you guys *might* remember that I was the one who caught Alan Gray when we thought he was the Phantom Phone Caller."

"Excuse me," said Claudia, "but you did not do it by yourself. *I* was there, too. *I* called the police. *I* — "

"Okay, okay, okay!" said Mary Anne. When Mary Anne raises her voice, we listen. She hardly ever raises her voice.

Luckily for all of us, the phone rang then. I answered it.

It was Mrs. Pike, Mallory's mother.

"Oh, hi, Dawn," she said. "I'm glad you picked up. I have a special job and I wanted to offer it to you."

Oops, I thought. Another special job? "What kind of special job, Mrs. Pike?" I asked.

You will never in a million years guess what Mrs. Pike's job was, so I'll just tell you. Remember when Mallory said that if her sisters heard about the pageant, they'd want to enter it? Well, sure enough, Claire and Margo (who are five and seven) had heard, and they did want to enter. There was just one problem. Mrs. Pike wasn't going to be able to help them prepare for it. She was all tied up with some big volunteer project at the public library, and she didn't want to back out of her duties. So she wondered if I'd help the girls prepare. She was asking me because I live close by and would never need a ride over. And she was *not* asking Mallory, who, of course, would be the most convenient helper of all. She knew what Mallory thought about pageants. I guessed Mallory must be pretty outspoken on that subject.

"Well," Mrs. Pike finished up, "what do you think? This job would be a little different from most. You'd have to help the girls choose outfits, rehearse for the talent competition, learn to greet the judges, that sort of thing. I'll get all the information we need from the pageant committee." She paused. "This is not the sort of activity I'd usually approve for the girls," she went on, "but they're *dying* to enter, and I don't really see a good reason for them not to participate. I just hope they won't be too disappointed if they lose. . . . Are you interested in the job, Dawn?"

I thought for a moment. I *did* want the job. It sounded like fun, and I needed some fun. I didn't want to cause any more problems among us sitters, though. On the other hand, this might be my chance to prove just how good I was with kids. Certainly as good as Claudia. Imagine if Claire or Margo won the contest and became Little Miss Stoneybrook! Plus, I wouldn't mind irking Kristy just a little bit to get back at her for the induction ceremony.

"I'll do it!" I said to Mrs. Pike happily.

I got off the phone and told the others about the job. Their reactions were interesting.

Jessi rolled her eyes — at the thought of the sexist pageant, I guess.

Claudia and Mary Anne looked thoughtful.

Kristy looked cross. Very cross.

And Mallory clapped her hand to her forehead and moaned, "Oh, no. My sisters. My baby sisters. They'll be contaminated. They'll be brainwashed. If I become the sister of Little Miss Stoneybrook, I will absolutely die!"

# CHAPTER 4

Saturday

This afternoon I baby-sat for Karen, Andrew, and David Michael while mom and Watson went to an auction to buy a birdbath. Most people go to auctions to buy paintings or statues or Oriental rugs. My parents go for a birdbath. Oh, well. I've gotten way off the subject. So anyway, I was sitting. The kids and I were playing Let's All Come In. (It wasn't easy talking David Michael into playing.) Then the boys quit the game and Karen got upset, so I just happened to mention the Little Miss Stoneybrook pageant to her, and she wanted to enter. I mean, really wanted to enter. And she's going to, and I'm going to help her get ready for it, just like Dawn is helping Claire and Margo. Of course, the decision wasn't made quite as easily as it sounds here, but finally Watson and his ex-wife gave Karen permission. . . .

$U$s baby-sitters try not to play favorites among the kids we take care of, but it's no secret that Kristy's favorite charges are her brother David Michael, and her stepsister and stepbrother, Karen and Andrew. She doesn't see Karen and Andrew all that often, since they only spend every other weekend, every other holiday, and two weeks during the summer at Watson's house, but she sees them enough, I guess, and she really loves them.

Who wouldn't? Karen is this funny, daring, imaginative, outspoken six-year-old. She likes to tell wild stories and make up games. And Andrew is a shy, sweet, and adoring four-year-old. Then there's David Michael, who's seven. Sometimes he and Karen don't get along too well, but he's a good kid. Kristy has been a second mother to him. Her real father left so long ago that David Michael barely remembers him, and then her mom went back to work. So Kristy has taken plenty of care of David Michael over the years.

Anyway, not long after the newspaper article about Little Miss Stoneybrook, Kristy was sitting for the three kids. It was a Saturday afternoon, and as she mentioned in her notebook entry, her mother and Watson had gone

31

to some auction to bid on a birdbath. Why? I don't know.

As soon as they were gone, Karen said, "Let's play Let's All Come In." (Let's All Come In is a game she made up. You need about four — or more — people to play, and what you do is pretend you're guests at a fancy hotel. You get to dress up in wild outfits and be all different people.)

Ordinarily, David Michael does not like this game.

"It's for babies," he announced that afternoon.

"I'm going to play," Kristy told him.

"Yeah, but you get to be the bell captain. That's not such a stupid part. The bell captain doesn't have to dress up like countesses."

"Or dogs," added Andrew. As the youngest, he usually gets stuck with the worst roles.

"Well, you can be the bell captain this time," Kristy said to David Michael. "I'll play guests instead."

"I don't know . . ." he replied.

"Aw, come on, David Michael," said Karen. "It's raining out. What else will you do if the rest of us play Let's All Come In?"

David Michael frowned. He didn't have an answer for that.

So the game began.

David Michael, as bell captain, stood in the living room, which was the hotel lobby. He was supposed to talk to the various guests and direct them to their rooms.

Karen got to be the first guest. She dressed up as Mrs. Mysterious, on her way to a witch convention. Mrs. Mysterious was one of her favorite characters.

"Heh, heh," she cackled. "What a lovely, spooky convention it will be. Hundreds of witches. Maybe a ghost or a goblin or two. Well, what room am I in this time?" Before David Michael could answer, Karen went on, "I hope it's the Halloween Suite. I'm just *dying* to stay there again."

"Yeah," said David Michael, looking a little bored. He pretended to consult the hotel registration book. "It's the Halloween Suite, all right. I hope you like it. See ya later."

Karen gave him an exasperated look. "My *key*, please?" she said.

"Oh, right." David Michael slapped the spare key to the downstairs bathroom into her hand.

Mrs. Mysterious left the room and Andrew entered. For once, Karen had given him a pretty good part. He was dressed as a sailor.

"Hiya, mate," David Michael greeted him.

"Hiya, mate. I need a room for two nights.

33

Our ship just landed here. I want to be a, um, a . . ."

"A landlubber," Karen prompted him from the doorway. (While she was dressing Andrew up, she had told him a few things that sailors might say.)

"A landlubber," finished Andrew.

"Naw. Really?" replied David Michael. "Don't you want to be on the ocean again? Be in a storm? Maybe see some pirates?"

"Yeah, pirates!" Andrew answered excitedly. "Say, you want to come back to my ship with me?"

"Sure!"

"Hey!" cried Karen. That wasn't the way the game was supposed to go.

But it was too late.

"We'll be pirates ourselves!" David Michael went on.

"Wait! You're the bell captain," Karen said desperately.

"No, I'm not. I'm Old Bad John. And this is my co-pirate, Andrew the Awful. Come on, Andrew."

The boys ran out of the living room, Andrew shedding parts of his sailor costume on the way.

Karen looked at Kristy with tears in her eyes, which was unusual. Karen is tough, not a crier.

34

"Oh, Karen," said Kristy. She opened her arms for a hug, and Karen ran to her. "It's okay," Kristy murmured.

"No, it's not," Karen sobbed, her voice muffled against Kristy's shoulder.

Kristy patted her back.

"There are too many boys around here," said Karen, obviously thinking of Kristy's big brothers, as well as Andrew and David Michael. And probably mad that Andrew had chosen to play with someone other than Karen herself.

"Well, us girls will just have to stick together, that's all," replied Kristy. And that was what made her think of the Little Miss Stoneybrook pageant.

"Hey," Kristy went on. "Do you know what a pageant is?"

Karen pulled back and looked at Kristy. She gulped. She sniffed. She wiped her eyes. "Like Miss America?" she replied.

"Exactly."

"Where the beautiful, beautiful ladies dress up in sparkles and sit on pianos and sing songs?"

"Yes."

"I saw the Miss America pageant on TV."

"Well, guess what. There's going to be a Little Miss Stoneybrook pageant right here in town. You can be in it if you're a girl and you're five to eight years old."

Karen's eyes grew huge. Her tears stopped. She began wiggling all over like a puppy. "Me! That's me! I'm five to eight! I mean, I'm six. Could I be in the pageant? Could I wear sparkles and stuff?"

"You'd want to be in the pageant?" Kristy asked her, just to make sure.

"Yes, yes, yes! What would I have to do?"

"Well, for one thing, you'd need some sort of talent. A talent show is part of the contest."

"I could sit on a piano and sing! Or I could tap dance, or — or twirl a baton, or make a doll talk."

"But Karen," Kristy said, "you don't know how to do those things. You've never taken lessons."

"I can sing!" Karen exclaimed. "Anyone can do that. Listen to this. *The wheels on the bus go round and round, round and round, round and round. The wheels on the bus go round and round.* Oh, you know the rest, Kristy. A million verses. *The driver on the bus says, 'Move on back, move on back.'* I could make up more verses. And what do you mean, I can't tap dance?"

Karen found her black patent leather party shoes and stomped across the wooden floor of the hallway. "See?" she said. "I can too tap dance."

Kristy told Karen about the beauty and poise parts of the pageant and meeting the judges and everything.

Karen grew more and more excited. "If I win I get a crown, right? And maybe a big bunch of roses?"

"Well, don't count on winning," replied Kristy. "I mean, you just never know." But then she went on, "If you *did* win, you'd get to be in another pageant, the county pageant."

"Oh, I just *have* to be Little Miss Stoney-brook!" cried Karen. "I have to!"

I suppose that at that moment, Kristy felt like I did when Mrs. Pike offered me the special job with Claire and Margo. Here was her chance to prove how great she was with kids.

So when her mother and Watson came home later with their birdbath, she and Karen told them about the pageant.

"Please can I be in it?" Karen pleaded. "Please, please, please? With a cherry on top?"

"Oh, honey," said Kristy's mother. She glanced at Watson. "I hate the idea of beauty pageants. Won't you be disappointed if you don't win?" she asked Karen.

"With a cherry and whipped cream and nuts

on top?" was Karen's reply. "I'll get to sing and everyone will watch me."

Watson shrugged. "If that's what she wants, I don't see what harm could come from entering her in the contest. I'll have to check with her mother first, though. And, Kristy, are you prepared to take the responsibility of getting Karen ready for the pageant?"

"Oh, *sure*," replied Kristy, thinking that (as far as she was concerned) that was half the point.

So Watson called his ex-wife and they talked things over. They decided Karen could enter the Little Miss Stoneybrook pageant.

Kristy and Karen were both thrilled.

When I found out, I was nervous. I felt as if suddenly the contest had become Claire, Margo, and me against Kristy and Karen.

## CHAPTER 5

"I'll clear the table," said Jeff.

It was dinnertime, and Jeff had been un-usually helpful ever since Mom had said she'd see if he could go back to California after all. Helpful and pleasant.

"That's okay. It's my turn tonight," I replied, jumping up.

"No, no. I'll do it." Jeff was already on his feet.

I glanced at Mom, who was still picking at her eggplant. She hadn't eaten much that night, although she'd seemed to be in a good mood. She'd told us all about a baby shower that had been held that day at the company where she works. One of Mom's friends was going to have a baby in a few weeks.

"It was fun," she'd said, "but by the time it was over, I thought if I heard one more person say, 'Oh, isn't that *cute?*' I'd get sick. That's what everyone kept saying. Each time Kelly opened a present, we all said, 'Oh, isn't that *cute?'* Even *I* did. Even when she opened the gift *I* gave her!"

Jeff and I had laughed.

Now I watched Mom poke at her food.

"You all finished?" asked Jeff. He was hovering at Mom's elbow. The rest of the table had been cleared.

Mom put her fork down. "Yup. All done. The eggplant wasn't very good, was it?" she asked.

"It was fine," Jeff and I replied together.

"Thank you for being such polite children," said Mom with a smile.

"Hey, am I completely off the hook tonight?" I asked hopefully. "If you don't need me in the kitchen, then I'll go start my homework."

"I don't need you in the kitchen," Mom answered, "but I need you in the living room. Jeff, too. I want to talk to you."

Jeff and I glanced at each other curiously. "Right now?" I asked.

Mom looked around the kitchen. She sighed. "Sure. Right now. This mess can wait, I suppose."

Jeff and I followed Mom into the living room. She indicated that we should sit on the couch.

We sat.

Mom sat in a chair facing us.

40

She smoothed her hair back from her face. "Well," she began, rubbing her hands together nervously, "I don't know how to say this except just to *say* it. Jeff, we've worked everything out. You may go back to California and try living with your father for six months."

Jeff was so stunned that he couldn't even answer, but I could see excitement written all over his face. There was no way he could hide it.

And how did I feel? Shocked, that's how.

"Mom, you *didn't!*" I exclaimed.

"Didn't what?"

"Go through with it."

"Honey, you knew I was going to. Or that I was going to try to, anyway."

"When do I leave?" Jeff wanted to know.

"Well, not for a little while. But as soon as all the arrangements have been made. There's still a lot to do. I mean, aside from packing, there are papers to be drawn up and signed, I've got to send your school and medical records back to California, your dad has to find a housekeeper, and he'll have to re-enroll you at Vista." (Vista was the school Jeff and I had gone to in California.)

"How long will all that take?" Jeff said.

"A couple of weeks, I guess."

"Only two weeks? All *right!*" Jeff's excitement was growing. He wouldn't be able to contain it much longer.

I understood how he was feeling. But I wasn't feeling anything at all myself. I was numb. Once, I had an infected finger. A splinter had gone in and I couldn't get it out. My father said he would try to get it out for me. Before he started "operating" he held an ice cube on my finger to numb it. That's how I felt now. As if someone had applied a giant ice cube to my body. And to my brain, as well.

"I can't believe you're letting him go," I said harshly to Mom.

"I don't think I have much choice," she said.

"Yes, you do. People always have choices. And you're making this one."

"Okay," agreed Mom. "Maybe you're right. But I think it's the best choice."

"How can it be the best choice when it hurts so much?"

Jeff was looking back and forth from Mom to me as we spoke. He looked like he was watching a game of Ping-Pong.

"Right choices aren't necessarily easy ones," Mom countered.

"They should be," I said crossly.

"I'm sorry, honey."

I paused.

Jeff looked at me. "Your turn," he said. He smiled, but I didn't smile back. Nevertheless, Jeff couldn't contain himself anymore. He leaped off the couch. He kissed my mother. He went jumping around the room. "All *right!* All *right!*" he kept shrieking. "Thanks, Mom! Just think — no more Ms. Besser, no more Jerry Haney, no more fights or trouble or homesickness."

"Thanks a lot," I said to him.

"What do you mean?"

"You won't be homesick for us? You mean that when you're in California you won't miss us anymore? That's nice, Jeff. That's real nice. You are so, so thoughtful." I bit my lip to keep from crying.

"Aw, come on, Dawn. Can't you be happy for me?"

"No!"

"Dawn, try to understand — " my mom began, but I cut her off.

"I understand plenty. Jeff can't wait to get out of here. He can't wait to leave us behind —"

"It's not that," Jeff broke in. "That's not true at all. It's just that nothing's working out. I don't belong here."

"You don't belong with your own mother and sister?" I asked incredulously.

"I belong with Dad, too," he replied. Then he grinned. "I gotta call the Pike triplets. They won't believe this. And then, Mom, can I call Jason?" (Jason is one of Jeff's California friends.)

"Sure," replied Mom.

I threw myself against the cushions of the couch and sulked. I felt guilty. I felt guilty because there I was, making a fuss over Jeff's leaving, when I wouldn't have minded going right along with him. He wasn't the only one who missed Dad. I did, too. And I missed my friend Sunny, and I missed the kids I used to baby-sit for. Face it. I wanted to go back to California, too. But I wouldn't leave Mom. No way. We were much too close for that. Besides, I liked Stoneybrook, too. Even in the middle of the freezing cold, snowy, icy winter, I liked Stoneybrook. What I wished was that we hadn't moved at all. Then I wouldn't feel so confused.

"Dawn?" said Mom gently.

"Yeah?"

"I know you're upset. This must be tough on you. It's more than just the fact that Jeff's leaving, isn't it?"

I nodded. "I miss California, too — Oh, but I want to stay here," I assured her. "But I do miss Dad and Sunny and good old Vista. . . .

Mom, don't you feel hurt that Jeff is so excited about leaving us?"

"I don't think he's so much excited about leaving us as he is about getting back to California. He's relieved to be leaving Connecticut behind. That's not quite the same as wanting to leave *us*."

"I guess not."

Mom sat down next to me and pulled me to her. She stroked my hair. "I've told you this before, sweetie. Jeff *will* miss us. Once he's back in California he'll miss us. And he'll want to visit us. But I don't think he'll want to live with us. His experience here has not been good. And that wasn't our fault and we can't change what's happened."

"I know," I said finally. "I guess I'm just . . . sad. I wish there were some way to keep him here."

"Oh, we could keep him here, all right," Mom told me, "but it would be like keeping a wild bird in a cage. Unfair. And the bird would be unhappy. Do you understand?"

"Yes," I replied. "I don't like it, but I understand."

Mom kissed me on the forehead. "We're going to be fine, you and I," she said. "You were my first baby, my special girl."

"Sometimes," I said, "I feel more like your sister than your daughter."

"Funny. I feel more like your sister than your mother."

We smiled ruefully at each other.

"I think I'll go to my room," I said.

Mom nodded.

"On second thought, I'll go to your room. If Jeff's off the phone can I call Mary Anne?"

"Of course."

In Mom's room I dialed Mary Anne's number. I hoped she would keep her head when I gave her the awful news. Mary Anne cries so easily that sometimes you wind up comforting her when it should be the other way around.

But Mary Anne was great. She said she knew how awful I must feel. She said the arrangement stank. She said Jeff was being selfish. Her voice only wobbled once.

When I got off the phone I went to my room and closed the door. I flopped on my bed. I began to cry, but before I really let go, I hastily wiped my tears away.

I started to think about Claire and Margo and the pageant instead. I was supposed to work with them the next day. I wondered what they could do. Sing? Claire knew her brother Nicky's silly song about jingle bells and Batman smelling, but I wasn't sure what else. Margo was hopelessly uncoordinated, so dancing and baton-twirling were out of the question. She could stand on her head, but that probably didn't qualify as talent. Maybe I could teach her a song on the piano. (The Pikes have a grand piano.) And maybe Claire knew some other songs. I hoped so.

I would find out the very next day.

# CHAPTER 6

I went over to the Pikes' house right after school. Just to refresh your memory, the eight kids are: Mallory (eleven); Adam, Jordan, and Byron (the ten-year-old triplets); Vanessa (nine); Nicky (eight); Margo (seven); and Claire (five).

There are very few rules at the Pikes', but one is that if more than five of the kids are at home when the parents are out, then *two* sitters must be there. On that day, Mr. Pike was at work (he's a lawyer for some company), and Mrs. Pike was busy with her library project. Since the triplets had stayed at Stoneybrook Elementary for after-school sports, and I was going to be working with Claire and Margo, Mallory was left alone in charge of the remaining two kids — Vanessa and Nicky. She was already on duty by the time I got there, having rushed home from school so that her mother could get going.

Claire and Margo greeted me at the door in great excitement.

"Hi!" cried Claire. "Hi, Dawn-silly-billy-goo-goo!" (Claire can be very silly at times. It's a phase she's going through.)

"Are you here to help us?" asked Margo, jumping up and down. "With the pageant, I mean? We can't wait!"

"We love to get dressed up!" added Claire.

"Hey, Claire! Margo!" I could hear Mallory call. "Let Dawn in, for heaven's sake. She can't help you if you leave her standing outside."

"Come in come in come in come in come in!" shrieked Margo.

Oh, brother, I thought. As my dad would have said, the girls were wound up tighter than ticks. (Which, when you think of it, doesn't make much sense. How do you wind up a tick?)

I entered the Pikes' hallway. Mallory came out of the kitchen, smiling.

"Hi, Dawn," she said.

"Hi," I replied. "Listen, I really hope you don't mind that I'm, um . . ." (I didn't want to humiliate the girls, but what I meant was that I hoped Mal didn't mind that I was getting her sisters ready to be the embarrassment of her life.)

"Well," said Mallory slowly, figuring out what I meant, "you know how I feel about . . . this, but it *is* your job, and besides, Claire and Margo are so excited."

Were they ever! They were sashaying around the living room with their hands on their hips, looking like . . . I'm not sure what, exactly.

"Why don't you take them up to their room?" Mallory suggested. "You can have some privacy there, and besides, Mom said something about looking through their closet. We haven't gotten the official rules from the judges' panel yet, so we don't know the details about the pageant, but we do know that . . . Let's see. What did Mom say? Oh, yeah. They need a sort of party outfit for this parade in front of the judges and the audience, and another thing to wear in the talent competition, and a third, but we don't know what yet."

"Bathing suits!" shouted Margo.

Mallory smiled. "No. This isn't Miss America, Marg. There's no swimsuit competition."

"I want to wear my bathing suit!"

Mallory raised her eyebrows as if to say to me, "See what a pain in the neck this pageant's going to be?"

I sighed. "Come on, girls. Let's go upstairs and see what's what."

The girls thundered up the stairs ahead of me.

"Good luck!" Mallory called.

"Thanks," I replied.

Claire and Margo raced into the bedroom they share. Before I could say a word, they opened their closet and began peeling their clothes off. Margo reached for her bathing suit. On the front was a gigantic alligator, its mouth open in a grin full of big triangular felt teeth.

"This is what I'm wearing," she announced.

"For what?" I asked.

"The *pageant*," Margo replied impatiently.

"But what part of the pageant? You heard Mallory. I really don't think you'll need a bathing suit. Listen, the first thing we'll pick out is a fancy outfit for the parade. Won't it be fun to get all dressed up?"

"Like for church?" asked Claire.

"Well, or for a birthday party," I replied.

"But I don't wear sparkly dresses to birthday parties or church," said Claire. "The ladies on TV wear sparkles. Or fur. I need to do that, too."

"Claire, you don't *need* to," I said desperately. "You don't need bathing suits, either," I added, glancing at Margo. "Look, let's forget about your clothes for awhile. We can choose those any time. Why don't you get dressed again? Then you better start thinking about the talent show. Because you'll have to rehearse whatever you decide to do. Do you guys know what rehearse means?"

"Choose?" asked Claire.

"It means practice, dummy," Margo told her.

"Margo," I admonished her.

Claire stuck her tongue out at her sister. "Silly-billy-goo-goo!"

"Okay, that's enough," I said. "Now listen. What do you want to do in the talent show?"

"What are we supposed to do?" Claire asked.

"Whatever you're good at. Most people sing or dance or play an instrument. Or they twirl a baton or do acrobatics. The talent competition is like a variety show on TV. What can you do?"

The girls looked thoughtful.

"Do you play the piano?" I asked them.

"I play the kazoo!" exclaimed Claire.

"I can play 'Chopsticks' on the piano," said Margo. "Jordan taught me."

I shook my head. Then, "How about dancing?" I asked, knowing that Margo, at least, was hopeless.

Claire put her arms in the air. She twirled

around and around, got dizzy, tripped over a teddy bear, and fell down.

"What about singing?" I asked after I had kissed her bumped knee.

"I can sing," said Margo. (Claire was sniffling and rubbing her knee.) "We sing all the time in music class at school. Listen to this. It's the song about the smart reindeer: Rudolph the Red knows rain, dear."

"Margo," I said when she had finished. I paused to think. Margo was giggling away at her reindeer joke, but there was a little problem. She couldn't carry a tune. She might have been singing any song. Any song at all.

"What?" asked Margo.

I tried to be tactful. "I don't think Christmas songs are quite right for the pageant."

"Then *I'll* sing," Claire declared, jumping to her feet, apparently recovered. "This is my best song, and this is what I'll sing in the pageant: *I'm Popeye the sailor man. I live in a garbage can. I eat all the wor-orms and spit out the ger-erms. I'm Popeye the sailor man.*"

Claire smiled sweetly at me.

I sank onto her bed.

"That's it," said Claire firmly. "That's my talent."

There was no changing her mind. At least,

I thought, trying to be optimistic, Claire can carry a tune. And she *can't* do anything else. "Are you sure you don't want to sing a different song?" I asked her, just to be sure. "Like 'Tomorrow' or 'Somewhere Over the Rainbow'?"

"No, Dawn-silly-billy-goo-goo. That's my best song."

Well, maybe we could dress her in a little sailor suit or something.

"Okay, Margo. Let's think about your talent again," I said. And suddenly inspiration hit. "Hey, you could recite something!" I suggested. "A nice long poem like 'The Owl and the Pussycat.'"

"I know 'The House That Jack Built'!" Margo cried. "This is the house that Jack built. This is the malt, that lay in the house that Jack built. This is the rat, that ate the malt, that lay in the house that Jack built."

Margo wasn't sure of the rest of the poem, but she found her book called *The House That Jack Built*, and decided she could memorize it.

"Terrific!" I told her.

But Margo was frowning. "It doesn't seem like enough," she said. "It's just talking. It's — Hey, I know! I know something I can do *well* that I've never seen anyone else do. It's real talent! I'll be right back."

I looked at Claire. "Do you know what she's going to do?" I asked her.

"Probably the banana trick."

The banana trick? My stomach began to feel funny. . . .

Margo returned to the room carrying a banana. "Watch this!" she exclaimed. She sat on the floor, leaned back against her hands, picked up the banana with her feet — and peeled it with her toes.

(And I thought she was uncoordinated!)

"This is the house that Jack built," she said, after the banana had been peeled. She took a big bite. "Thish ish the mart, that ray in the housh that Jack bit."

"Shee?" she said a few moments later, as she polished off the last of the banana. "I can peel a banana with my feet. I bet no one else can do that. And I can eat it while I say my poem."

I closed my eyes. I thought I felt a headache coming on. I didn't feel any better when I heard Claire say, "My talent is better than yours, Margo. I'm going to win the pageant."

Of course Margo replied, "No you're not. *I* am."

What next? I wondered. It hadn't really occurred to me that the Pike girls would be competing against *each other*. What if one of them did win the pageant? The other would lose not just to strangers or even friends, but to her own sister. How awful!

On the other hand, I was beginning to think that there wasn't much chance that either girl *would* win — not with banana-peeling and rude Popeye songs.

"You guys," I said, "let's go on to something else. You're probably going to need to know how to curtsy. I bet you'll have to curtsy when you meet the judges. How about practicing that for awhile?"

The girls looked at me blankly. "What's curtsy?" asked Margo.

I explained.

I demonstrated.

The girls tried curtsying.

Margo tipped over sideways. Claire knelt down so low she had trouble getting up.

"Let's work on poise," I suggested. I placed a book on each girl's head. "Now stand up straight and walk gracefully, just as if you were walking by the judges."

Margo did so, batting her eyes and looking coy.

Claire did so, too, but she swayed her hips back and forth and the book slid to the floor.

"Told you," said a voice from the doorway.

It was Mallory. She looked disgusted, but her sisters didn't seem to notice.

"Watch our talents, Mallory-silly-billy-goo-goo!" Claire cried.

Mallory watched. (Margo had to demonstrate without a banana, though. I didn't want her to spoil her appetite for supper.)

When Claire and Margo were finished, Mallory glanced at me. It was all we could do to keep from laughing. Nevertheless, as I walked home that evening I began to wonder what I'd gotten myself into.

The Pike girls were not pageant material at all.

# CHAPTER 7

Thursday.

Guess what, everybody. We have another contestant in the Little Miss Stoneybrook pageant -- Myriah Perkins. And all the other contestants better watch out because, boy, is she talented. She can sing, tap dance, and act, and she knows ballet. She's taken lessons for all these things. Oh, she also knows gymnastics. She can turn a cartwheel and stand on her head and do a backward somersault and some other stuff. I am not kidding. Really. I'm not.

Myriah didn't know anything about the pageant, but when I saw how talented she is, I just knew she'd have to enter. She'll win, too. I'm sure of it.

When I read Mary Anne's notebook entry I smelled trouble. Big trouble. The pageant business was getting out of hand. Or maybe it wasn't. Maybe I was just disappointed that the Pike girls were going to peel bananas and sing about wor-orms and ger-erms. At any rate, Myriah suddenly seemed like hot competition.

The Perkins family lives next door to Mary Anne. They live in the house Kristy lived in before her mother married Watson Brewer and the Thomases moved into his mansion on the other side of town. There are five people in the Perkins family — Mr. and Mrs. Perkins, five-and-a-half-year-old Myriah, two-and-a-half-year-old Gabbie, and Laura, the newest member of the family, who's just an infant.

The afternoon that Mary Anne sat at the Perkins house was a gloomy, rainy one, but Myriah and Gabbie didn't seem to mind. (Mary Anne was sitting just for the two older girls while their mother took Laura to the doctor for a checkup.) They had dressed up in funny clothes and were dancing around their playroom.

"*On the goo-oo-ood ship* Lollipop," Myriah sang, "*it's a something, something, something to the candy shop, where bonbons play, something,*

*something on Peppermint Bay.* . . . Stop, Gabbie. Wait," Myriah said. "Where . . . hmm . . . *And if you eat too much — ooh, ooh — you'll awake with a tummy ache.* . . . Gabbers, hold on. Let me finish."

Myriah was trying to remember the words to a song she had learned the year before. She wanted to perform all by herself, but Gabbie kept pulling at her arm. "Let's sing 'Silent Night,'" she cried.

"No, Gabbers. It's not Christmas. And I'm trying to remember this song."

*"Si-ilent night,"* Gabbie sang anyway. She strutted across the floor in an old pair of clumpy high-heeled shoes.

"You know," Myriah told Mary Anne, "if I could just remember the words to this song, I could sing it and tap dance to it. I took lessons last year. I wonder if my tap shoes still fit."

Myriah dashed out of the playroom.

Gabbie followed her. "I'm coming, too. I'll look for my baldet shoes. I can be a baldet dancer!" she called over her shoulder to Mary Anne.

In a few minutes, the girls returned. Gabbie returned quietly in a pair of pink ballet slippers that had once belonged to Myriah. Myriah returned noisily. "They fit!" she exclaimed.

"My tap shoes still fit! Now watch, Mary Anne. Okay?"

"Okay," replied Mary Anne. I bet the wheels were turning even then. I bet Mary Anne was mentally auditioning Myriah for the pageant.

Myriah rolled back a throw rug and stood on the wooden floor. She held her arms to one side, smiled, and began stepping across the room. In time to the tapping of her shoes, she sang, *"On the goo-oo-ood ship* Lollipop, *it's a something, something, something to the candy shop, where bonbons play —"* She paused. "I don't think that's right, Mary Anne. Not just the something–something part, but even the bonbons part. Oh, well."

"Well, I'm sure we could find the words printed somewhere. But can you sing any other songs?" asked Mary Anne, knowing full well that she could. Both Gabbie and Myriah are famous in the neighborhood for all the long songs they know.

"I know 'Tomorrow,' " replied Myriah. "You know, from *Annie*? But I can't tap dance to it."

"Let me hear it anyway," said Mary Anne.

(Gabbie was dancing a slow, graceful ballet in a corner of the room, lost in her own world.)

"Okay, here goes." Myriah gathered herself together. Then she belted out, *"The sun'll come out tomorrow. Bet your bottom dollar that tomorrow, there'll be sun. . . ."*

She sang the entire song. She knew every word, was right on pitch, got the timing right, and even added a few hand gestures.

Myriah had an amazing voice.

Mary Anne was impressed. She was so impressed that she told Myriah about the Little Miss Stoneybrook pageant.

"And you think I could be in it?" Myriah asked, awed.

"Sure," replied Mary Anne. "Why not?"

"I don't know," Myriah said slowly.

"Have you ever seen a pageant before?" Mary Anne asked her. "On TV or something? Like Miss America or Miss Universe?"

"Yes," replied Myriah.

"Well, wouldn't you like to be in one for girls? You'd get to dress up and sing or dance. And if you won, you'd wear a crown."

Myriah wasn't saying anything, but her eyes were growing rounder by the second.

"Could I be in it, too, Mary Anne Spier?" asked Gabbie. (She calls everyone by their full names.) Gabbie had stopped dancing. She came over to the couch, where Mary Anne was sitting, and climbed into her lap.

"Oh, Gabbie, I'm afraid not," Mary Anne told her. "You have to be five years old to be in the pageant. You have to be five or six or seven or eight. And you're two."

"I'm almost three," Gabbie said hopefully.

"I know, but you need to be five."

"Yuck, yuck, yuck," Gabbie replied, sliding out of Mary Anne's lap. But she didn't seem too upset.

"You know," said Myriah excitedly, "there are lots of things I could do in the pageant. I know ballet for real. I mean, I've taken lessons. Gabbie just plays in my old shoes. She won't take lessons until she's three. But I know all the positions and I can dance to 'Waltz of the Flowers.' I know gymnastics, too. And I can act! I took creative theater. I was the baby bear in *Goldilocks and the Three Bears.* I had to say, 'Who ate my porridge?' and 'Look who's sleeping in my bed!' and some other stuff."

Mary Anne was as excited as Myriah by then. "We'll have to ask your mom about the pageant, though," she reminded her. "You'll have to work in order to get ready for it. And you might need some new clothes."

Both Mary Anne and Myriah were on pins and needles waiting for Mrs. Perkins and the baby to come home. As soon as they did, Mary Anne, Myriah, and Gabbie all rushed to them.

"What a welcoming committee," said Mrs. Perkins with a smile.

"I missed Laura Loo, Mommy," Gabbie said.

"And Mary Anne wants to ask you something," Myriah spoke up.

"Yes?" said Mrs. Perkins as she unzipped Laura's little jacket. She placed the baby in an infant seat.

Mary Anne nervously explained about the pageant and said she'd help Myriah get ready for it. She wondered if maybe she should have mentioned it to Mrs. Perkins before she got Myriah all excited. What if Mrs. Perkins said no?

As it was, she didn't say yes right away.

Mary Anne and Myriah glanced at each other.

"Please can I be in it?" Myriah asked. "Mary Anne will help me."

Mrs. Perkins frowned. "Yes, you can be in it, honey — " she began.

"Hurray!" shouted Myriah.

"— and I'll be happy for Mary Anne to work with you. But I want you to remember something. I want you to think about this."

"Okay."

"You, too, Mary Anne," said Mrs. Perkins. Mary Anne nodded.

"In any pageant, or in any game or contest, there are winners and there are losers. You might be a winner, Myriah, and that would be wonderful. Daddy and Gabbie and I and even Laura would be very proud of you. But you might be a loser, too. There are going to be lots more losers than winners. And I want you to know that we'll be proud of you if you lose. We'll be proud of you for having the courage to be in the pageant, and for the work and rehearsing you'll do."

"I know," said Myriah, giving her mother a hug. "Thank you."

"One more thing," said her mother. "I think you should know that for some girls, this pageant won't be just fun and games. I hope it'll be fun for you, but for others it will be work. They'll take it very seriously. You might be competing against girls who have been winners in other pageants, or who have won beauty contests or talent contests. They'll know how pageants work. And they might — just *might* — not be very friendly. I want you to understand what you're getting into, that's all. Okay?"

"Okay," said Myriah. She smiled happily. (She was missing four teeth.)

Myriah really *had* listened and paid attention to what her mother said. But Mary Anne hadn't. Not much anyway.

As it turned out later, she should have. So

should all of us baby-sitters. We kept talking about how winning wasn't important — and not one of us really believed it. The fact is, Mary Anne knew — she could feel it — that *she* was going to be the one to sponsor the winner of the Little Miss Stoneybrook crown. She would prove that she was the best baby-sitter of all.

# CHAPTER 8

Friday

I taked to Stacey today! I know that dosn't have a thing to do with baby siting but I just wanted to tell you guys. I mean becuase Stace used to be one of us. And Charlitte talked to her to. maybe I shold start at the begining. See I sat for Charlite Johassin today she misses Stace just like I do. So I said come on over to my room and well call Stace. So we did. Gues what hapened when we were their. Charlitte found the paper whith the article abot the Little miss stoneybrook pagent in it and she is going to enter. I hope she realy whants to since it was my idea but Dawn your helping the Piks and Kristy your helping Karen and mary Anne now your helping maria so I'm going to help Charlitte. We'll see what we see.

Claudia had been sitting for Charlotte quite a bit. Not as often as Stacey had sat for her, but a lot. On Friday afternoon, she showed up right after school. Charlotte greeted her at the door with, "Did you bring the Kid-Kit? Did you bring the Kid-Kit?"

Claudia hadn't. She felt terrible. She was sure Stacey would have brought the Kid-Kit.

"I'm *really* sorry, Char," she said. "I was — "

"And we were right in the middle of *Mr. Popper's Penguins*, too."

Actually, that may have been one reason (a subconscious reason, if you know what I mean) that Claudia hadn't brought the Kid-Kit. She may have forgotten it on purpose. Claudia is not a great reader. Her favorite books are Nancy Drew mysteries. But Charlotte is this smart, smart little kid who has skipped a grade and may actually be a better reader than Claudia. Even so, she loves to be read *to*. Imagine Claudia having to spend a lot of time reading out loud. Oh, well.

The point was, Claudia didn't have the Kid-Kit with her, and she felt bad and so did Charlotte. Charlotte is an only child who's a little shy and doesn't see her parents that much. They love Charlotte to bits, but her mother is a doctor and her father has some other important job so they're both just very busy.

Claudia tried to take the sting out of forgetting the Kid-Kit. "Are you playing with Becca a lot these days?" she asked. (Becca is Becca Ramsey, Jessi's little sister. The Ramseys moved into Stacey McGill's house, which is close to Charlotte's.)

"Yes," said Charlotte, and she lowered her eyes.

"But?" Claudia prompted her.

"Well, I just can't help it," Charlotte blurted out. "Every time I go over to her house it reminds me of Stacey."

"Oh," said Claudia. "That must be hard. I know you miss Stacey."

"Yeah," Charlotte agreed. "I do."

"So do I. She was my best friend."

'She was my best friend, too," said Charlotte.

"You know what I miss most about her?" Claudia asked.

"What?"

"I miss how she was just always *there*. You know what I mean?"

"I'm not sure," Charlotte replied honestly.

"Well," said Claudia slowly, "I mean that I could call her any time for any reason. I could go to her with any problem. Or with any good thing that happened. I could count on her for fun or help or sympathy or anything. I guess that's what a best friend is."

"Exactly!" cried Charlotte, sounding grown-up. "We had fun together, but sometimes Stacey helped me with problems. And a couple of times *I* helped *her!* Really."

"I believe you," said Claudia.

"Boy, do I miss her."

"Yeah."

Claudia and Charlotte were beginning to feel pretty depressed. Claudia told me that they were just sitting on the floor in the living room. Charlotte was picking at the rug, and Claudia was pulling at a thread on her pants. Luckily, Claudia got an idea that she knew would cheer both of them up.

"Hey!" she cried. "I know! Let's go to my house and call Stacey!"

"Really?" said Charlotte, looking up excitedly. "We could really *call* her? I could *talk* to her?"

"Sure! I call her all the time. My phone bill gets pretty big, but I earn enough money baby-sitting to pay for the calls to New York. So let's go!"

"Oh! Oh, Claudia, I love you!" As Claudia and Charlotte got to their feet, Charlotte threw herself around Claudia in a fierce hug. "I love you," she said again. "This is great. Let's go!"

70

Claudia scribbled a note to Dr. and Mr. Johanssen telling them where she and Charlotte were, just in case one of them should come home early. Then she and Charlotte threw on their jackets and ran most of the way to the Kishis' house.

They arrived panting and out of breath, greeted Mimi, and ran up to Claudia's room.

"Where's the phone?" was the first thing Charlotte asked, looking around Claudia's bedroom.

The thing about Claudia is not that she's a slob exactly (Kristy's the slob), but that she's a pack rat. Since she loves art, she's always collecting things that might come in handy with her projects — interesting leaves, scraps of paper and fabric, corks, sponges, bottle caps, you name it. So sometimes it's hard to spot things amid the clutter. Plus, you never know what you might find buried somewhere.

Claudia knew right where her phone was, though, and she dialed Stacey in New York. Of course, she had long ago memorized Stacey's number.

Charlotte perched on the edge of Claudia's bed while they waited for someone to answer the phone. "Oh, I hope she's there, I hope she's there," she whispered over and over.

*Click.*

"Hello, Stace?" said Claudia. (Charlotte's eyes lit up.) "Hi, it's me! I want to talk to you, but there's someone here who wants to say hi first."

Claudia handed the receiver to Charlotte. "Hello?" Charlotte said nervously. "Hi — Stacey? It's Charlotte. Charlotte Johanssen. . . . Yes! Oh, I miss you, too! I miss you so much!"

Claudia watched Charlotte's face as she spoke to her beloved Stacey. She had never seen her happier. Charlotte told Stacey about school and friends and Becca and some books she'd read. At last she said, "I guess I better let you talk to Claudia now, huh? . . . Yeah, she *is* a good sitter. She baby-sits me a lot." (Charlotte smiled at Claudia.) "Okay. . . . Okay. . . . Yeah. . . . I love you, too. 'Bye, Stacey."

Charlotte gave the phone back to Claudia. While Claudia and Stacey were talking, Charlotte poked through the junk that was all over the room. After she looked through a box of scraps and a folder full of sketches and watercolors, she came across a copy of the *Stoneybrook News*. She settled down with it, turning the pages slowly.

Guess what the first thing she said to Claudia was when Claudia had finished her phone call. She said, "Look at this. It says here there's going to be a pageant in Stoneybrook. The judges are going to choose a girl to be Little Miss Stoneybrook."

Charlotte had found the old copy of the paper, the one with the article about the pageant!

At that, Claudia raised her eyebrows. She felt left out, not having a kid to prepare for the pageant like Kristy and Mary Anne and I did.

"Yeah!" said Claudia eagerly. "It's for girls ages five to eight. *You* could enter, Charlotte."

*"Me!"* Charlotte exclaimed. "What for?"

"Don't you think it would be fun?"

"Not really. I'd rather read."

"If you won you'd get a crown and everyone would make a fuss over you and you'd probably get your picture in the paper."

"You're kidding!"

"Nope. And guess who else is going to be in it — Margo and Claire Pike, Myriah Perkins, and Karen Brewer. You know, Kristy's little sister."

"They are?"

"Yup. Wouldn't you like to be in it, too?"

"I don't know. What would I have to do?"

Claudia told her about the poise and talent and beauty stuff. "The talent competition is really important," she added. "What can you do?"

"Nothing," Charlotte said flatly.

"Nothing? Don't you take music lessons at school or something?"

"No. And I've never taken ballet or gymnastics."

"Can you sing? Almost everyone can sing."

"No way. Especially not in front of a whole bunch of people. All I can do is read. . . . Hey! Maybe I *could* read. You know, give a — what do you call it? — a dramatic reading. Or I could memorize something from a book — like the part in *The Wizard of Oz* when the cyclone comes. That is so, so scary. Or I could recite the part in *Charlie and the Chocolate Factory* where Violet Beauregarde turns into a giant blueberry. That's really funny."

"You know," Claudia said slowly, "that's not a bad idea. It's not like singing or dancing; it's different. The judges might like it. Do you want me to ask your mom if you can be in the pageant?"

Charlotte scrunched up her face in thought. "I don't know," she said. "See, the thing is, I'm not pretty."

"Being pretty isn't the point," Claudia told her. "It really isn't. You have to have poise and talent and be smart."

"But you have to be pretty, too. I know you do," Charlotte replied.

Claudia didn't answer her right away. The thing is, Charlotte is quite pretty, with big dark eyes and chestnut-colored hair, but Claudia knew how useless it is to try to convince someone that she's pretty when she thinks she's not. So all she said was, "This isn't just a beauty show, Char. I guarantee it."

It took a little more talking, but finally Claudia convinced Charlotte that they should ask if she could be in the pageant. Claudia knew she didn't have a very confident participant, but at least she had one.

And when they talked to Dr. Johanssen about it, she gave them her permission, along with the other usual stuff. She said that Claudia would take the responsibility of preparing Charlotte, and that Charlotte should try not to be *too* disappointed if she lost.

So the Little Miss Stoneybrook pageant gained another contestant.

# CHAPTER 9

If Jessi and I have to hear the words "This is the house that Jack built" one more time, we are both going to have nervous breakdowns. We sat at my house for my brothers and sisters this afternoon, and Claire and Margo spent hours rehearsing. Now everyone in the house has that poem memorized.

*Yeah. Here's the last verse: This is the farmer who sowed the corn, that fed the cock that crowed in*

Stop it, Jessi, I can't stand even to see it written.

*I'm sorry, Mal, but I'm sort of proud of myself.*

Well, we're getting way off the subject.

*I know. Okay, you guys, here's the baby-sitting stuff: I arrived at Mallory's house at 1:30, just as her parents were leaving. Mal and I were going to be taking care of her brothers and sisters until about 6:00....*

I had no idea how caught up Claire and Margo had become in the pageant. I had told Mrs. Pike I would work with them a few afternoons after school. But apparently they were rehearsing and preparing on their own. As you can tell from Jessi and Mal's notebook entry, they spent all Saturday afternoon working on pageant stuff. I guess it got kind of annoying for Jessi and the Pikes. On the other hand, nobody gave the girls an easy time. According to Jessi and Mallory, this is how the afternoon went:

When Jessi arrived, the Pikes had just finished eating lunch. Nevertheless, Margo, who was standing in the middle of the living room, was holding a half-eaten banana in one hand and the copy of *The House That Jack Built* in the other (in case she forgot the words). She was rehearsing away in the banana-scented room.

"Thish ish the housh that Jack" (chomp, chomp, swallow) "built. This is the malt that lay in the" (bite, chew, chew) "housh that Jack bit. Thish ish the rat that — Oops." A piece of banana had broken off and fallen on the carpet.

"Ha, ha, ha! Hee-hee!"

Margo had an audience consisting of everyone in the house — Jessi, Mal, the triplets,

Vanessa, Nicky, and Claire. A few of the kids began to laugh when the banana fell apart.

"Mal, don't you think she ought to rehearse in the kitchen?" Jessi said. "It's awfully hard to get banana out of a rug. I know because Squirt smushed a big piece of one into the carpet in the den last week. I thought Mama was going to have a fit."

"Good idea," Mallory replied. "Margo, you better rehearse in the ki — Don't *eat* that! Don't you dare put that in your mouth!" she cried as Margo aimed the fallen piece of banana toward her lips. "It's been on the floor."

"Ew, ew, ew!" cried Claire.

"Ew, ew, ew!" mimicked Nicky.

"Aw, do I have to go in the kitchen?" asked Margo.

"Just until the banana is gone," Mallory told her. "And after that, no more bananas. You can't rehearse with them all afternoon. You'll make yourself sick. Concentrate on the poem."

"Boo," replied Margo unhappily, but she headed for the kitchen anyway.

Everyone followed her. They all wanted to watch.

Margo stood in front of the refrigerator. She popped a piece of banana in her mouth and chewed it thoroughly.

Just as she was about to begin reciting, Adam

jumped in with, "This is the mouse the cat killed. This is the fly that landed on the mouse the cat killed. This is the spider that ate the fly that landed on the mouse the cat killed."

"Adam!" Margo cried. "Mallory, Jessi, those aren't the right words! Make him stop!"

"Adam," said Mallory warningly.

"Mallory?" Adam replied.

Mallory hid a smile. She thought Adam's poem was sort of funny. And she thought all the pageant business was ridiculous. But as a baby-sitter, it was her job to try to keep the peace. She frowned at Adam. He frowned back, but remained quiet.

"Thish ish the housh that Jack" (swallow) "built," said Margo.

"This is the fly that landed on the mouse the cat killed," Adam continued for her.

"*Adam!*" screamed Claire and Margo.

"Why don't you go rehearse in your room?" Jessi suggested to the two hopeful beauty queens.

"No!" they shrieked. "Make Adam be quiet."

"Adam — " Jessi began.

"Never mind," he said hastily. "Come on, you guys," he added, and as he left the kitchen he was followed by Jordan, Byron, Nicky, and Vanessa.

Mallory and Jessi looked at each other and

shrugged. Then they left, too. Claire and Margo were alone in the kitchen.

"Good," said Margo with satisfaction. "Now we can really rehearse."

"Right," agreed Claire. "Only it's my turn to 'hearse."

"No, mine! I'm not finished."

"It's *mine!* I haven't even started."

"*Mine!*"

"MINE!"

"Okay, break it up in there!" shouted Mallory from the living room. "Either take turns or rehearse in separate rooms."

Margo and Claire looked at each other. Margo had finished her banana. "Separate rooms," she said, glaring at her sister.

"*Good*," said Claire angrily.

As Margo marched out of the kitchen she called over her shoulder, "I'm going to win, you know. Because my talent is better than yours."

"Is not!" Claire began singing at the top of her lungs, "*I'm Popeye the sailor man. I live in a garbage can.*"

"Claire, hold it down just a *little*," said Jessi, poking her head into the kitchen.

Claire ignored her. "*I eat all the wor-orms and spit out the ger-erms. I'm Popeye the sailor man!*"

From the rec room, Margo began an even

louder rendition of her poem, starting with the long last verse: "THIS IS THE FARMER WHO SOWED THE CORN, THAT FED THE COCK THAT CROWED IN THE MORN, THAT WAKED THE PRIEST ALL SHAVEN AND — "

"*STOP!*"

Utter silence reigned in the Pike house.

Jessi, who had never raised her voice in front of the Pikes, had had enough. "If you two can't rehearse quietly, then go outside," she said firmly.

"Better yet, don't rehearse," added Mallory, coming to Jessi's side. They were standing at the entrance to the kitchen. Mallory was looking in at Claire. Jessi was looking down the steps at Margo in the rec room.

"We'll be quiet," said Margo contritely.

"Yeah," agreed Claire.

For half an hour, the girls did rehearse quietly. And separately. Then Margo tiptoed up the steps to the kitchen, carrying her copy of *The House That Jack Built*. "Claire?" she said sweetly. "Let's work together, okay? There are a few things I could show you. Like how to shake hands and stuff."

"I know how to shake hands," Claire replied. Still, she looked pleased that her sister wanted to help her.

"Do you know the special Judges' Hand-shake?" asked Margo.

"Judges' Handshake?" Claire repeated. "No. I thought Dawn said we would curtsy for the judges."

"Well, we'll probably have to shake their hands, too, and you better know how to do it. Here, hold out your left hand."

"But I thought — " Claire began.

"Right hand for regular people, left hand for judges," Margo interrupted importantly.

"Margo! Cut that out!" called Mallory. "You're making that up!"

"Are you?" asked Claire, sounding wounded.

"Yeah," Margo admitted.

"Then you go back downstairs and 'hearse alone," said Claire. "Oh, but first would you get me a glass of milk, please? Since you were so mean to me?"

"Oh, all right."

Margo poured out a glass of milk and handed it to her sister. "Hey, where's my book?" she asked, looking around for *The House That Jack Built*.

Claire gazed at Margo with wide, innocent eyes. She blinked. "I don't know."

"You do too. You hid it!"

"Did not!"

"Did so!"

Jessi had to step in to break up the latest fight. When the girls had settled down and Claire had returned Margo's book (which she *had* hidden), Jessi marched them into the living room, where Mallory and the rest of the Pikes were involved in a hot Monopoly game.

Mallory tried to find something quiet for Claire and Margo to do. "I hate to suggest this," she said, "but why don't you girls practice your poise or something. Practice walking like . . . walking like . . . Oh, I can't even say it."

"I can," spoke up Jordan. "Practice walking like gorillas."

"Jordan!" shouted Claire and Margo.

"How about walking like, um, females?" suggested Jessi.

"We could try the books again," Claire said to Margo.

"Use encyclopedias," said Nicky.

The girls ignored him. They each found a small paperback and began sashaying around the living room with the books on their heads.

"Oh, that is pathetic," said Mallory to Jessi. "Look at them. They're going to think the only thing that matters in their lives is beauty and poise. They'll grow up believing they can only be pretty faces, not doctors or lawyers or authors."

"I am so glad Becca has stage fright," said Jessi.

At that moment, Adam got to his feet. He followed his sisters around the room, wiggling his hips and singing in a high voice, *"Here she comes — Miss A-meeeer-i-ca!"*

Claire and Margo didn't utter a word. They just threw down their books and stomped out of the living room. Claire went to the kitchen, Margo to the rec room. A few moments later, the Pikes and Jessi heard, *"I'm Popeye the sailor man . . ."* all mixed up with, "This is the farmer who sowed the corn . . ."

"I have a headache," commented Mallory.

"Me too," said Jessi, Adam, Byron, Jordan, Vanessa, and Nicky.

They moved their Monopoly game upstairs and waited for the afternoon to end.

# CHAPTER 10

This is the house that Jack built. This is the malt that lay in the house that Jack built. This is the rat —

Stop! Stop! Stop!

I was having a stupid conversation inside my head. I couldn't get that darn poem out of my mind. It was with me all the time.

This is the farmer who sowed the corn, that fed the cock . . .

Claire's song was with me, too.

*I eat all the wor-orms and spit out the ger-erms I'm Popeye the . . .*

Ew, ew, ew.

"Dawn, would you pay attention, please?"

I jumped. Thank goodness I wasn't in school, just at a meeting of the Baby-sitters Club. Even so, Kristy looked about as peeved as a teacher who's caught a kid drifting around in outer space.

85

"Sorry," I said. "It's that poem that Margo's going to recite in the Little Miss Stoneybrook pageant. It's driving me crazy."

"*Tell* me about it," said Mallory. She looked a little wild.

And Jessi immediately added, "This is the farmer who sowed the corn, that fed the cock that crowed in the morn, that waked the priest all shaven and shorn . . ."

Mallory and I joined in with, "That married the man all tattered and torn — "

The phone rang then and Kristy reached for it, saying, "Amazing," and giving us a look that might have meant she thought we were totally demented, or might have meant she was really, really impressed with us. It was hard to tell.

Kristy took the call and lined up a job for Mallory with Jamie Newton, this little kid our club sits for a lot. When she was finished, she said, "So. I guess we've each got a kid entering the pageant now. I mean, except for you guys," she added, looking at Mallory and Jessi.

Our junior club members were sitting side by side on the floor, leaning against Claudia's bed and making necklaces out of gum wrappers. Mary Anne and Claudia and I were lounging on the bed. Kristy, of course, was sitting straight and tall in the director's chair, her visor in place. She reminded me a little of an army sergeant.

"Yeah," said Mallory. "We wouldn't be caught dead doing something like that. . . . Oh, I'm sorry! Really I am. I didn't mean to insult anybody. It's just — I meant — I meant — "

The rest of us were laughing, though. I was glad Mallory felt comfortable enough with us to say something like that. And I couldn't resist replying, "It'd be pretty hard to enter a kid in the pageant if you were dead, wouldn't it?" I said.

Mallory began to laugh, too.

"Well," I went on, "how's everybody coming along? Claire and Margo will be ready for the talent show, if nothing else."

There was a moment of uncomfortable silence.

I tried again. "Claudia, what's Charlotte going to do in the talent show?"

Claudia looked down at her hands. Her gaze traveled right on down to Mal and Jessi on the floor. "I used to make gum chains," she said. "I had a whole ensemble — a necklace, three bracelets, an ankle bracelet, even earrings."

What kind of answer was that?

I turned to Kristy. "What's Karen going to do?"

More silence.

"How's Myriah coming?" I asked Mary Anne.

(Mary Anne got very busy examining the tip of a pen.)

"What *is* this, you guys?" I finally exploded.

"Charlotte's talent is a secret," Claudia replied haughtily.

"So's Karen's," said Kristy.

"And Myriah's," added Mary Anne.

"I thought Myriah was singing and tapping to 'The Good Ship *Lollipop*,' " I said.

"Maybe and maybe not. She has so many talents. She could act or tumble or do a ballet routine, too."

"You mean you haven't decided yet?" said Kristy, looking both smug and hopeful.

"Oh, we've decided," Mary Anne replied. "I just don't want to say anything."

"No fair!" I cried. "You *all* know what Claire and Margo are doing."

The other girls shrugged as if to say, "Tough luck."

The phone rang three times in a row then, and we lined up jobs for Jessi, Claudia, and me. When our business was finished, and Mary Anne had recorded everything safely in the record book, I ventured another question.

"Did Karen and Myriah and Charlotte receive the pageant information?" (A fat envelope had arrived in the Pikes' mail a few days earlier. It had contained everything we'd need in order for the girls to be official contestants. There were forms to fill out and several pages describing the pageant, what would go on, and exactly what the girls would need to prepare for.)

"Yup," said the others, and Kristy added, "I've already sent Karen's forms back." She looked pleased with herself and quite proud.

But Claud, Mary Anne, and I all said, "So did I."

"Oh," said Kristy.

"The questions look hard," spoke up Mary Anne.

"Which questions?" asked Claudia.

"The ones the girls have to answer at the end of the pageant. You know, the last category they receive scores in."

"Oh, yeah," I said. "All those questions like, What is your greatest hope? and, If your house were burning down and you could rescue three things, what would they be?"

"Now *that* sounds interesting," said Mallory, looking up from her gum chain.

"Yeah," agreed Jessi. "Something their brains will actually be involved in."

"That's right," said Mary Anne. "I'm preparing Myriah very carefully."

"Preparing her?" I repeated. "What do you

mean? How can you prepare her? We don't know what the questions will be. That's one area where the girls'll just have to wing it."

"No way," Kristy jumped in. "You have to get the girls thinking of peace and good will and humanity. Mushy stuff like that. You don't want Margo saying she'd rescue money and toys and her Cabbage Patch doll from a burning house. You have to get her thinking along different lines. She better say she'd rescue any family members she could find, her dog or cat — "

Kristy suddenly stopped talking, as if she realized she'd given away state secrets or something.

"Oh, brother." Mallory clapped her hand to her forehead. "They're even ruining this part of the pageant," she said to Jessi. Then she looked at the rest of us. "Wouldn't you rather see the kids use their heads? Be creative? I'd like to see one say she'd rescue the photo album so she'd still have memories."

"Or rescue a lucky penny so she could wish for everything back," added Jessi.

I hardly heard them. I was lost in thought. I hadn't even *told* Claire and Margo about the questions they'd be asked. I'd mentally picked out their outfits for that part of the pageant, but that was all. Now I realized they'd have to "rehearse" answering questions.

The meeting was interrupted then when my mom called with a non-job question. She'd been doing that a lot lately.

"What's up?" asked Mary Anne as soon as I'd gotten off the phone. She was the only one of my friends who knew what was going on in my family, and she looked worried.

"Mom is, um . . . I don't know. Her question was really unimportant. It could've waited until I got home. I think she just wanted to hear my voice."

"Why?" asked Kristy.

I glanced at Mary Anne. Then I looked around at my friends. "I might as well tell you," I began, and my voice must have indicated that it was something serious. Everyone grew quiet. Jessi and Mal put their gum chains down.

"What's wrong?" asked Claudia in a hushed voice.

"Jeff's going back to California. Not just for a visit. For real."

"Forever," said Mal, nodding her head, and I realized then that *she* probably *did* know the news. Jeff had told the triplets.

"Well, he's going back for six months. It's supposed to be a trial, but I have a feeling it'll turn into forever."

"Why?" asked Jessi, who didn't know too much about my family yet. "Who's he going to stay with?" She looked frightened, like she thought we were giving Jeff away or something.

"Oh, my father," I assured her. "And this is his choice. He's the one who wants to go. But, well, I just don't think we'll feel much like a family anymore."

Jessi nodded sympathetically.

"How did your dad get custody?" Kristy wanted to know.

I told them the whole story, from Ms. Besser's fateful phone call until right now. "Now" was Jeff's stuff slowly being packed away into trunks. It was my mom crying in her room at night. It was me crying in my room at night. It was all of us, even Jeff, feeling like we were going through the divorce again. And because of that, it was Mom clinging to me, as if to say, "Don't you go away, too."

Well, I wouldn't. That was the one thing she'd never have to worry about.

The meeting ended and we went home.

# CHAPTER 11

It was Friday, my last chance to work with the Pike girls. The next day was Saturday — the pageant! But before that, that very night, Mom and I would put Jeff on a plane back to California. We weren't certain when we'd see him again.

I tried not to think about that. I threw myself into the last-minute preparations for the pageant instead.

"Now today," I told Claire and Margo just after I'd arrived, "we're going to have a dress rehearsal. Do you know what that is?"

The girls shook their heads.

"Okay. It's when we pretend you're actually *in* the pageant. We'll go through the whole thing. You'll pretend to meet the judges, be in the beauty parade and the talent show and everything, and you'll even change your clothes so you'll be wearing the right outfits at the right times. That's why it's called a *dress* rehearsal. Get it?"

"Got it."

"Great. Now the very first event," I said, referring to the information the pageant people had sent, "is the walk across the stage when you meet the judges. It's the first time the audience will see all you contestants. Now Claire, you'll be wearing your blue dress for that, and Margo, you'll be wearing your daisy dress."

"Please can I wear my bathing suit?" begged Margo.

"Absolutely not."

"How come?"

"Because no one else will be wearing a bathing suit. The judges want you guys all dressed up."

"Okay, okay."

"Now tomorrow," I said, thinking aloud, "we'll have to make sure you've got your com*plete* outfits with you. We'll have to remember socks, shoes, slips, barrettes, everything you'll need." I hoped I could handle it. The pageant was beginning to seem like a huge job. There were times when I was sorry I'd taken it on. At least Mrs. Pike would be able to help me. She was going to help us before the pageant, and then drive us to the high school.

The girls put on their outfits and I led them down to the living room.

"What you'll have to do first thing is walk across the stage in the auditorium. All the judges except the head judge will be sitting in the first row of seats. The head judge will be on the stage. So what you do is walk toward the head judge. Remember to look at the audience and *smile* while you're walking. Before you get to the judge, say in a nice loud voice, 'My name is Claire Pike and I'm five years old.' Margo, you, of course, will say, 'My name is Margo Pike and I'm seven years old.' You'll curtsy and then shake her hand. Remember to use your right hand. That's the wristwatch hand." (Claire can't tell time, but she always wears a watch on her right wrist.) "Anyway," I went on, "shake her hand and remember to *keep smiling*. When you're finished, walk the rest of the way across the stage.

"Now let's try it. I'll be the judge, and that's the audience over there." I pointed to the dining room.

In the middle of our rehearsal I heard the Pikes' phone ring. A few moments later, Mallory called to me, "Dawn, it's Mary Anne!"

"Hold on, you two," I told Claire and Margo. "I'll be right back."

I ran into the kitchen and took the receiver from Mallory. "Hello?" I said. "Hi, Mary Anne. What's up?"

"Well, I was just wondering . . . I guess, um . . ."

"What were you wondering?" I asked impatiently.

"Um . . . um . . . How are the girls doing?"

"Fine. Are you with Myriah?"

"Yes."

I had a funny feeling that Mary Anne wasn't wondering anything except how Myriah's competition was doing.

"Listen," I told her. "We're really busy. We're right in the middle of a dress rehearsal, so I gotta go."

"A dress rehearsal? Oh, great idea! Thanks, Dawn. 'Bye!"

*Darn*, I thought. I'd given something away. The pageant was getting entirely too competitive. It wasn't fun anymore.

I returned to Claire and Margo. Even though I knew that when you hold a dress rehearsal, you're supposed to go from the beginning to the end of a show without stopping, I decided that we'd have to work on each event a few times (except maybe for the talent part). The girls had forgotten to smile when they walked toward me, and Claire kept losing her balance when she curtsied.

"Okay, let's take it from the top," I said professionally. "Claire, you first."

Claire pranced across the living room toward me.

"Smile!" I hissed.

She put on a huge, silly grin.

"Not that much. A regular smile."

Claire toned her smile down and said, "I'm Claire Pike, I'm five years old, and I really want to win. I have seven brothers and sisters, a mommy — "

"Whoa, whoa! All you say is your name and age," I reminded her. Why, oh, why had I ever told Mrs. Pike I'd prepare the girls for the pageant?

The rehearsal continued. When the girls were tired of curtsying, I said, "Let's move on. The next part of the pageant is the talent competition."

"Oh, goody!" said Margo. "My favorite part."

The girls ran upstairs and changed into their second outfits. I had to admit that those outfits were pretty cute. Mrs. Pike and I had taken the girls shopping one day and bought this adorable white sailor outfit and sailor cap for Claire to sing her Popeye song in. For Margo, we'd bought a pair of painter's pants in which we'd stuck a toy hammer, screwdriver, and paintbrush, to make her look as if she were Jack, the house-builder. Margo had wanted a monkey suit to go with her banana, but all the monkey suits had monkey feet, and I pointed out that Margo needed her feet free in order to peel her banana.

We returned to the living room.

"Okay," I said, "for this event, you wait backstage for the announcer to introduce you. When she's finished you walk to the middle of the stage — "

"Smiling?" interrupted Claire.

"The whole time," I told her. "I think there'll be an X marking the center of the stage. So you walk to the X and just do your number. When you're finished, the audience will start clapping." (I hope, I hope.) "Then you curtsy and walk off the stage in the other direction. Don't go back the way you came because the next contestant will be coming out from there and you'll run into her. Margo, why don't you go first this time. Oh, and since it's a dress rehearsal, use a real banana."

"What about the rug?" she asked as she ran to the kitchen for a banana.

"We'll risk it," I replied. "Okay. I'll be the

announcer." I cleared my throat. "Our next contestant is the lovely and talented Margo Pike, age seven!" I cried.

Margo, banana in hand, walked to the middle of the room, smiling like a pro. She sat down, put the banana between her bare feet, and peeled it in record time. Then she stood up, smiled, bit the top off the banana, and said, "Thish ish the housh that Jack bit. Thish ish the . . ."

I wanted to put my hands over my ears, but I managed not to.

Margo was reciting the last stanza of the poem, when I glanced at the entrance to the living room and realized that we had an audience.

Claudia and Charlotte!

"Aughh!" I shrieked. "Claire, Margo — *hide!*"

But Margo wasn't stopping for anything. She was almost done. ". . . that milked the cow with the crumpled horn," she said frantically, "that tossed the dog, that worried the cat, that — "

I grabbed Margo by the arm, hauled Claire off the couch, where she'd been waiting for her turn to perform, and yanked both of them into the dining room, out of view.

"Stay there!" I ordered them.

I ran back to the living room. "What are you doing here?" I demanded of Claudia. "And how did you get inside?"

"Vanessa told us we could come in. She's playing in the front yard."

"Well, what do you want?"

"We just wanted to see how you were doing." Claudia sounded kind of meek.

"Oh, that's fine. You won't tell me what Charlotte's talent is, but you'll come over here to spy on us."

"We're not spying!" said Charlotte indignantly.

"Besides, everyone knows what Margo and Claire are doing," Claudia pointed out. "You said so yourself."

"You didn't know about their costumes, though." I paused thoughtfully. Then I said, "Charlotte, I'll bet you have a *real* nice costume."

"Oh, it's *beau*tiful," she said. "Claudia and I made it. It's all — "

Claudia clapped her hand over Charlotte's mouth.

"Wmphh, wmphh, wmphh," Charlotte finished up.

"Pretty sneaky," Claudia said to me.

"So are you."

Claudia took her hand away from Charlotte's mouth.

"Are you going to have a fight?" Charlotte asked us worriedly.

Claudia and I looked at each other. "No, of course not," I said, relaxing a little. "I'm sorry I got so upset."

"And I'm sorry we came over and interrupted you," replied Claud. "I guess we *were* sort of spying. We'll get going now." Claudia looked as tired and as rattled as I felt.

"Okay," I said. "See you tomorrow. Good luck, Charlotte."

"Thanks," she said. "And good luck, Claire and Margo!" she yelled toward the dining room.

"Thanks!" the girls shouted back.

As soon as Claudia and Charlotte were gone, I called to Claire and Margo, and we got back to work. Margo started the poem over from the beginning, which nearly killed me, but I knew she wanted to rehearse.

Then it was Claire's turn. She sang her song once through and then began a little dance I'd taught her. I'd made it up myself, but it looked sort of like the sailor's hornpipe. When she finished the dance, she sang the song again — with hand gestures. She demonstrated dropping dangly worms into her mouth and spitting out their germs. She made horrible faces. It was pretty funny. Maybe she'd win in a humor category or something.

I helped the girls change clothes once again — into their outfits for the beauty parade. These outfits were the most dressy, and the girls looked great. They were wearing velvet dresses. The dresses were old hand-me-downs from Mallory and Vanessa, I think, but they were in beautiful condition. Since they were actually Christmas dresses, Margo's was green and Claire's was red. Each had a lace collar.

The girls rehearsed walking and smiling some more.

Then I said, "Okay, the very last event of the pageant will be questions, one for each girl. You'll stay in these outfits for that part. Now start thinking about nice, good, helpful things, and I'll ask you some questions. Okay?"

"Okay." The girls were sitting side by side on the living room couch. They looked tired, but determined. I hoped they could hold up during the pageant. The next day would be a long one.

"Margo," I said, "What is your greatest wish?"

"Global peace," she replied immediately.

"Yes, but say it in a *nice* sentence."

"My greatest wish," Margo said, looking rapturous and angelic, "is for global peace. That would be very . . . *nice*."

I only hoped the judge wouldn't ask her to explain what she meant. Margo didn't have the vaguest idea what global peace was.

"Great," I told her. "Now Claire, if the house were on fire and you had time to rescue three things, what would they be?"

"I would rescue," Claire began sweetly, "my family members, global peace, and the fire extinguisher."

I sighed. Claire and I had a lot of work to do. But I didn't mind. It kept me from thinking about what was going to happen that evening.

# CHAPTER 12

Claire and I talked and talked about how to answer those questions. I decided she was in pretty good shape when I said to her, "How could you change the world to make it a better place?" and she replied, "I would help everybody get to be friends and I would give them all free French fries at McDonald's."

Close enough.

Anyway, it was 5:30 and time to go home.

I said good-bye to the Pikes and walked home with as much enthusiasm as if I were walking to my own execution.

"Jeff?" I called as I entered our house.

"Hi! Hi, Dawn! I'm upstairs!"

Jeff was ecstatic and I was a mess.

I went up to Jeff's room and looked around. Jeff was sitting on his bed, grinning. (He'd been grinning for days.) His room looked the way it did right after we'd moved in and hadn't unpacked yet: bare. Most of his things had been put in trunks or cartons and shipped back to California. All that remained was a suitcase full of the clothes he'd been wearing the past few days and a knapsack that he was going to take with him on the plane that night. It contained a couple of books, a Transformer, his Walkman, some tapes, and a few things I could categorize only as junk.

Jeff was sitting on his bed looking through a pile of colorful papers.

"What's all that?" I asked him.

"Good-bye cards," he replied. "Ms. Besser gave me a going-away party today, and everyone in my class had made a card for me. It was their homework last night. Ms. Besser assigned it while I was in the boys' room yesterday. The party was a surprise."

"That was really nice of Ms. Besser," I said.

"I think she's glad to get rid of me."

I looked at the cards. They all said things like, GOOD-BYE, JEFF, and GOOD LUCK, JEFF, and I'LL MISS YOU, JEFF.

My curiosity overcame me. "Where's Jerry Haney's card?" I asked.

Jeff sorted through the pile and handed one to me. On the front it said simply GOOD-BYE, JEFF. But inside, in the middle of a complicated drawing, in letters so tiny Ms. Besser wouldn't have noticed them, were the words AND GOOD RIDDANCE.

"I'm taking all the cards with me — except Jerry's," Jeff told me. I watched him tear Jerry's card to bits and throw the pieces in his trash can.

"Hi! I'm home!" called my mother's voice.

"Hi, Mom," Jeff and I replied automatically.

"Come on downstairs," she said. "We have to eat an early, fast dinner."

"Okay!" I shouted.

"Dawn, can you carry my knapsack?" Jeff asked as he stuffed the cards in it. "I'm all packed. I might as well take my stuff downstairs when we go."

Jeff didn't even give his room a good-bye glance as he left it. Maybe boys don't care about those things. . . . Or maybe Jeff hated his life in Connecticut so much that he didn't want to remember it.

Jeff's last dinner with us was leftovers. "Sorry," said Mom, "but it's the fastest kind of dinner to have. I want to leave for the airport in forty-five minutes."

"I can't believe you're letting me take a night flight," Jeff commented happily as he shoveled in a forkful of reheated brown rice.

"I can't, either," said my mother. "But I

think it's the easiest way for you to go, in terms of jet lag. You'll leave here around nine — "

"I know, I know. And arrive at eleven o'clock California time."

"Right. You can sleep a little on the plane, and you'll still be able to get in a pretty good night's sleep in California."

"That is, if Dad and I don't stop to do something fun."

Mom and I exchanged a glance. "Jeff," Mom said seriously, "don't expect life with your dad to be like your vacation with him."

"I won't," he replied. But he still looked awfully excited.

Didn't he have even mixed feelings about leaving Mom and me? Didn't some tiny part of him think, Gosh, I'm going to miss Mom and my sister?

I had a feeling that the answer to both questions was no. And I was very, very hurt.

That night we didn't bother to do the dishes. We just cleared the table and put everything in the sink. Mom was nervous about the drive to the airport. "You never know about traffic jams," she said.

We were on the road before 7:00.

I let Jeff sit up front with Mom. I figured she'd have last-minute things to say to him like, "Obey Dad," or "Don't forget to lock the door if you use the restroom on the plane," or "Call us anytime. Call collect if you want."

But the ride to the airport was silent except for when a car cut in front of us and Mom hit the horn and muttered something I couldn't hear.

We reached the airport an hour before Jeff's plane was supposed to take off. As we stood in the white light of a streetlamp in the parking lot, I saw Mom blinking back tears. I glanced at Jeff, who was busy hauling his suitcase and knapsack out of the trunk of the car. He was whistling.

I took Mom's hand and whispered, "It'll be okay." Then I gave her a quick hug.

*Crash.* Jeff slammed the trunk shut.

"Okay, let's go!" he cried. "Can I buy some candy from a vending machine, Mom? Please?" (Jeff's one health-food downfall is chocolate.) "And can Dawn and I take our pictures in the photo booth? You get four. We could give two to Dad and you could keep the other two."

"Now, I *like* that idea," Mom told him. She smiled. It was hard to stay upset around someone who was so cheerful.

We walked into the airport and checked Jeff's suitcase through.

"I hope it actually ends up in California," I

said, "and not in Albuquerque like the last time we visited Dad."

"Oh, well," said Jeff mildly, "it'll get to California some time. And my other stuff should be there by now. Right, Mom?"

"Right."

"Just think," said Jeff as we wandered toward a gift shop. "I'll have my old room back. *My* room. The room here was never *my* room."

"Of course it was," I said sharply. "Who'd you share it with?"

Mom put her hand on my shoulder, silently telling me to calm down.

"Nobody," Jeff replied. "It just wasn't mine the way the one in California is. I can't explain it."

"Let's look in this store," said Mom, not too subtly changing the subject. "Do you need anything for the flight, honey?" she asked my brother.

Jeff looked thoughtful. "I don't think so. I've got two books and my Walkman, and anyway, I'm supposed to go to sleep," he added, glancing slyly at Mom. "But could I get a Mars Bar from a vending machine?" Jeff just loves vending machines and photo booths and those machines that plasticize things for you.

"Sure," replied Mom. "We have time to kill."

We found a corridor, luckily on the way to the gate from which Jeff's flight would leave, that looked like Vending Machine Alley.

"Oh, boy!" exclaimed Jeff.

"I hope you have a lot of change, Mom," I said.

She did.

Jeff bought a Mars Bar and tossed it in his knapsack. Then he and I squeezed into a photo booth and tried to smile and look grown-up as the camera took our pictures. The photos turned out quite well and we gave Mom first dibs on them. After the photo session, we still had time to kill, so Jeff plasticized nearly everything in Mom's wallet.

When he was done, Mom said, "We better get to the gate, kids. They may board you early, Jeff, since you're traveling alone. A stewardess will accompany you on the plane, and we've got to find her."

The gate was a mob scene. An awful lot of people were taking the night flight to Los Angeles. Jeff and I sat down while Mom spoke to a man behind the check-in counter. While we waited for her, I looked at my brother. He was rummaging through his knapsack. My baby brother, I thought, even though he was no more a baby than I was. Jeff and I may have had our share of fights, and Jeff may have been nearly impossible to live with lately, but he was my brother and I was going to miss him.

How could we let him go? Hadn't Jeff and I huddled together in my room in California during Mom and Dad's noisy fights? Hadn't I protected him from bullies and nightmares and imaginary monsters? Hadn't *he* taught *me* how to climb ropes when my gym teacher said I was hopeless? How could I grow up the rest of the way without knowing him?

"Don't go," I whispered.

"What?" said Jeff.

"Nothing."

Most families stay together. A lot don't — the parents split up. But in our case, we couldn't even keep the kids together. My insides were aching. And I knew that Mom felt like a failure.

My mother sat down with us to wait, and a few minutes later a stewardess approached. She smiled at Mom, then turned to my brother.

"Jeff Schafer?" she asked.

Jeff jumped to his feet, ready to go.

"I'm Elaine," said the stewardess. "I'll help you board now, and I'll give you any help you might need during the flight. Okay?"

"Sure!"

Mom and I stood up. The hugging and crying

started. All us Schafers were hugging, but Mom and I were the only ones crying. No tears fell from Jeff's eyes.

The stewardess watched us with some surprise. I'm sure she didn't know that Jeff had no return ticket. Most boys who leave their families plan to come back.

"Good-bye! 'Bye, Jeff!" Mom and I called as Elaine led him away.

When he was out of sight, I sank onto my chair. I was sobbing right in the middle of that crowded room. So was my mother. We held on to each other for dear life.

Mom tried, for the umpteenth time, to assure me that Jeff might not *think* he was going to miss us, but that he really would. I had trouble believing her.

When we calmed down, we linked arms and walked out of the airport together.

# CHAPTER 13

Pageant Day!

I was dead tired, not having slept much the night before. Even so, I was glad of the busy day ahead. It would be a long one, an exciting one, and I needed that in order to keep my mind off Jeff.

The pageant was to begin at 1:00. It would be held in the auditorium of Stoneybrook High School. But the contestants were supposed to be at the school by 11:30. I had told Mrs. Pike I'd come over to their house around 10:00.

At 9:45, as I was getting ready to leave, I said, "Mom, can't we call Dad and Jeff now? Just to make sure Jeff got there okay?"

"Honey, it's only a quarter to seven in California," she replied. "They'd kill us. Besides, if Jeff *didn't* get there we'd have had a frantic phone call from your father hours ago."

Mom was sitting at the kitchen table drinking coffee. She looked awful. I didn't think she'd slept at all the night before. I wasn't even sure she'd gone to bed, although she was in her nightgown and robe, and her hair was a fright.

"I know," I said. "You're right. Hey, Mom, why don't you come to the pageant today? I know you don't like the idea of them, but this one might be funny — I mean, fun — and you'll know a lot of the girls in it."

"Maybe I will," she replied.

"You could sit with Mr. Spier. He's going because Mary Anne helped Myriah Perkins get ready for the pageant." (My mom and Mary Anne's dad are old friends.)

"I'll think about it," said Mom, and she actually smiled. "Now you scoot."

I scooted.

When I rang the Pikes' doorbell, it was answered by Mallory, looking positively murderous.

"I hope you can calm Claire and Margo down," was the way she greeted me. "They are driving us bananas."

From upstairs I could hear, ". . . that kissed the maiden all forlorn, that milked the cow with the crumpled horn, that tossed the dog . . ." mingled with, ". . . *I live in a garbage can. I eat all the wor-orms . . .*"

"Just look at their room," Mallory added ominously as I started up the stairs. "Oh, by the way, Mom said to say she'll be up in a minute to help you."

"Okay," I replied.

I stood at the entrance to Claire and Margo's room. I swear, I thought an earthquake had hit. Hair ribbons and shoes and socks and barrettes and rubber bands were everywhere. The girls were trying to rehearse in the middle of the mess. The only good thought that came to mind was that, by the afternoon, the pageant would be over.

"*What* is going on?!" I exclaimed.

Claire and Margo ran to me.

"Oh, you're here!" cried Claire.

"Mommy said to get all our stuff together," Margo tried to explain. "And we were nervous. And we didn't want to forget anything, and . . ."

It took almost an hour, but Mrs. Pike and I managed to get the girls organized. First we dressed them in jeans and T-shirts for all the pre-pageant stuff. Then we laid out their outfits separately and put each one in its own bag — except for the dresses, which we placed on hangers to try to keep them neat.

"What else do we need?" asked Mrs. Pike, looking around.

"Curling iron!" I said.

We remembered a few more items, put them

in yet another bag, and were on our way to the high school. Mrs. Pike drove us. As we traveled through town I kept saying things like, "Remember to smile — all the time," "Remember to give *nice* answers to the questions," and "Don't worry if you forget your lines while you're performing. Just start over again or make something up. That's the professional thing to do."

Mrs. Pike dropped us off in front of the high school with her own set of reminders for the girls. She and the rest of the Pikes wouldn't see Claire and Margo again until the show started.

"We'll sit as close to the front as we can!" Mrs. Pike called as she pulled into the street.

The girls and I struggled into the high school building with our bags. Someone showed us to the auditorium, and we walked through a doorway labeled Stage Door.

Chaos. Pure chaos.

There were going to be fifteen contestants in the pageant, and most of them seemed to have arrived already. Backstage was a sea of little girls waiting to be told what to do. Some were rehearsing, some were checking their wardrobes, some were patiently having their hair curled or braided or brushed.

Claire and Margo immediately panicked.

116

"Look at that girl!" exclaimed Margo in a loud whisper. "She's wearing *nail* polish. *Daw-awn . . .*"

"*That* girl has *make*up on!" Claire added, not even bothering to whisper.

"Hey, there's Myriah," said Margo. She pointed across the room. "Look. She's tap dancing. And she's *good!* I mean, she's really goo — Oh, no! Oh, no, Dawn! Oh, *no!*"

"What! What?" I cried.

"Did you remember my banana?"

"*Yes.* It's in the bag with your painter's pants. Now will you two please calm d — " I stopped when someone tapped me on the shoulder. "Yes?" I said, turning around.

Behind me stood a stout woman with iron-gray hair piled high on her head. She was holding a clipboard. "Hello," she said warmly. "I'm Patricia Bunting, the pageant coordinator."

"Hi," I replied, shaking her hand. "I'm Dawn. This is Claire Pike and this is Margo Pike."

"Wonderful," said Ms. Bunting. She handed me a list. "Here's the order in which the contestants will appear onstage in each portion of the show. The order — youngest to oldest — will remain the same, so be sure Claire and Margo know whom to follow. As soon as everyone has arrived, I'll talk to the contestants. I'll explain how the pageant will run, and then I'll show them the stage. Mothers and big sisters will wait right over there," she went on, indicating an area in which folding chairs had been set up.

Claire and Margo looked at me, and we smiled. Ms. Bunting thought I was their sister!

Ms. Bunting walked away, and I sat the girls down so we could study the list together. "Let's see," I said. "Claire, you're near the beginning. You'll always go on stage right after Myriah. And Margo, you're sort of near the middle. You'll always go on right after Sabrina Bouvier."

"Right after *who?*" exclaimed Margo.

"Shh," I said. "A girl named Sabrina Bouvier."

Margo looked frantically around the backstage area. Her eyes traveled over Myriah, Charlotte, Karen, and several other contestants, and landed on the girl who was wearing the makeup (and plenty of it, I might add).

"That's her," said Margo fiercely. "I just bet that's her. Who else would have a name like Sabrina Bouvier?"

I didn't have an answer to that. Besides, I was trying to size up Claire and Margo's competition. There was Myriah, tapping away as Mary Anne watched her. Mary Anne looked exhausted but approving. No doubt about it, Myriah really was good. Her talent was true talent, not just some little act thrown together for the pageant. And there was Karen, looking awfully pretty. Kristy was nervously brushing her hair. And there was Charlotte, simply looking scared to death. She and Claudia were standing around awkwardly, almost as if they didn't even want to *be* there.

I caught Claudia's eye and we waved.

The girls waved to Charlotte and then ran over to her.

I followed them. "Hi," I said to Claud. "How are you doing?"

"Nervous. I'll be glad when this is over. It was a bigger deal than I thought it would be. How about you?"

"I'm a little nervous."

"I'm a lot nervous," I heard Margo tell Charlotte.

"I wish I'd never said I'd do this," Charlotte replied.

A new voice spoke up. "I can tell you how to get rid of the Pageant Jitters forever," it said, sounding as if it were reciting something from a TV commercial.

The voice belonged to the girl with the makeup.

"You can?" said Claire, Margo, and Charlotte in unison.

"Certainly. It would be my pleasure."

I glanced at Claudia. Who was this kid? She was about Margo's age, but she looked and acted twenty-five.

"How do you know how to do that?" Margo asked. "By the way, my name's Margo."

"I'm Sabrina," said the girl, and Margo shot me a look that plainly said, "I told you so."

Sabrina curtsied daintily. "So *very* pleased to meet you," she said in this funny, false voice. "This is my sixth pageant. That's how I know about the jitters." She was showing the girls some relaxing breathing exercises when a woman wearing tons of jewelry and even more perfume approached us. Her perfume reached us before she did.

"Come along, Sabrina," said the woman. "I want to try to introduce you to the judges."

Sabrina smiled sweetly at the other girls. "This is my mother. I really must run," she said. "There's always so much to do before a pageant. I do wish you the very best of luck."

Charlotte and the Pikes stared after Sabrina as Mrs. Bouvier whisked her away.

"Do you know what that was?" Claudia whispered to me. "A pageant-head, that's what. A poor kid who gets roped into any beauty contest or pageant that comes along. Her whole life is one big smile."

"She's not that pretty," I pointed out.

"And maybe not very talented," added Claudia. "But she knows pageants — or her mother does — and she knows what the judges like."

I was about to say that Sabrina's life might be one big smile, but it must be awfully boring, when Ms. Bunting clapped her hands together loudly. It was time for her to talk to the excited contestants. The girls gathered around her, and the rest of us drifted toward the folding chairs.

I sat with Claudia, Mary Anne, and Kristy, but none of us said much. We were getting awfully nervous. A whole bunch of butterflies were flapping around in my stomach.

I watched the girls as Ms. Bunting spoke earnestly to them.

I watched Sabrina's mother and some other mothers. While most of the mothers chatted or poked through their daughters' bags of clothing, Mrs. Bouvier glued her eyes on poor Sabrina and watched her intently.

Finally Ms. Bunting led the girls onto the stage. As soon as they were out of sight, the rest of us relaxed a little.

"Myriah looks good," I said to Mary Anne after a few minutes.

"Thanks," she answered. "She's rehearsed endlessly. She nearly had a heart attack this morning, though. She lost another tooth. It shook her up a little. I hope it won't break her concentra — "

Ms. Bunting and the girls returned and Ms. Bunting raised her voice. "The pageant will begin in exactly half an hour," she announced. "It's time to get ready for the first event of the afternoon — the introduction to the judges and the audience."

Claire and Margo ran to me.

"Time to get dressed! Time to get dressed!" cried Margo.

*"I'm Popeye the sailor man!"* added Claire.

I produced the girls' bags, and they began to change their clothes.

In just a few short hours, one of the girls now getting dressed backstage would be crowned Little Miss Stoneybrook.

# CHAPTER 14

As you can probably imagine, the talent show was the best part of the Little Miss Stoneybrook pageant, so I'll mostly tell you about that, but I won't leave you in the dark about the rest of it.

Picture this: You are backstage with a bunch of nervous mothers (or baby-sitters) and an even more nervous bunch of overdressed little girls. A heavy curtain separates you from an auditorium full of people — mostly the families and friends of the overdressed little girls. The curtain also separates you from the stage, on which is now standing an announcer who is saying, "Welcome to the first annual Little Miss Stoneybrook pageant, sponsored by the friendly folks at Dewdrop Hair Care, hair products for today's youth."

"What about next week's youth?" Kristy whispered to me.

I tried not to giggle.

The announcer went on to tell the audience how the pageant would work and how the judges would score the contestants. Then he introduced the judges (the owner of Bellair's Department store, the woman who ran the Stoneybrook Dancing School, and some doctor). After that, the head judge, a woman named Mrs. Peabody, joined him on the stage. Mrs. Peabody had once owned a charm school. Finally he said, "I'd like to send heartfelt good wishes to each and every little miss who is backstage right now."

"Oh, gag me," whispered Kristy.

Somehow, now that we were actually at the pageant, and it was as stupid as Mallory and Jessi had said it would be, I didn't feel quite so serious or competitive. I could tell Kristy didn't either. I was glad for that.

"The girls have worked hard," the announcer continued, "and I wish we could crown them all. Unfortunately, only one little miss will go on to Stamford to participate in the county pageant. She will receive a one-hundred-dollar savings bond and, of course, will be our grand winner. We will also select a first and second runner-up. The second runner-up will be awarded a fifty-dollar savings bond, and the first runner-up will be awarded a shopping spree in Toy City."

"Oooh," sighed every single contestant and every single child in the audience. I had to admit that the Toy City spree seemed like a pretty good prize. Even *I* would have liked it. I could get great stuff for our Kid-Kits.

"And now," the announcer continued, "it's time to meet our lovely contestants." He paused while somebody somewhere stuck a cassette in the stereo system, and a recording of marching music blasted into the auditorium, then was quickly turned down.

"All right, girls," said Ms. Bunting softly.

The contestants were lined up in their age order, and one by one, Ms. Bunting aimed them onto the stage, leaving just enough time for each to say her name and age, then curtsy and shake Mrs. Peabody's hand before sending the next one out.

There were three little girls in front of Claire. Just as I heard Myriah greeting the audience, I saw Ms. Bunting send Claire onto the stage. I didn't have a very good view of her, but I could hear her all right and this is what she said: "My name is Claire Pike and I'm five years old. . . . Oh, hi, Mommy! Hi, Daddy! Hi, Mallory! Hi — "

The announcer prodded Claire toward Mrs. Peabody, but Claire forgot to greet her and walked right offstage.

I groaned. Mary Anne, standing nearby, reached out and squeezed my hand. I looked at her gratefully.

Margo did better than Claire. She remembered everything, but she was nowhere near as dazzling as Sabrina Bouvier, who had been onstage just before her. Sabrina looked as if she might have been born on a stage. She smiled glamorously at the audience and the judges, curtsied prettily, and shook Mrs. Peabody's hand smoothly.

Okay, I thought, after all the little girls had been introduced. So Sabrina was gracious and sophisticated. So what? She might not have any talent at all. Or maybe she'd be really, really stupid and not able to answer her question. I didn't have much time to think about that, though. The talent show was beginning and I had to help Claire and Margo into their costumes.

Backstage was a madhouse. All around us were cries of, "My socks! Where are my *socks?*" or "Help! Fix my hair!" Here and there were little bursts of song. Not far away, I could hear Charlotte muttering something about giant blueberries and a girl named Violet.

I managed to get Claire into her costume just as the first contestant was winding up her rendition of "The Star-Spangled Banner," which

126

she was singing in a red, white, and blue sequined leotard. She had a terrible voice, like fingernails on a blackboard. (Claudia and I looked at each other and giggled.) Then I helped Margo with her painter's pants and handed her the banana.

The second contestant, who had sung a song which she'd written herself called "I Love My Dog," ran offstage — and Myriah ran on. She was wearing a pink leotard, a pink tutu, and her tap shoes, and she was carrying a gigantic lollipop. She looked calmly at the audience. Then out came her voice, clear and loud: "*On the goo-oo-ood ship* Lollipop . . ." And her feet went tappety-tappety-tap. I was extremely impressed. She looked like she should be on TV or something. When she was done the audience applauded loudly. They even cheered and whistled. Myriah smiled toothlessly and ran off. She was a hit.

"And now, Little Miss Claire Pike!" cried the announcer.

"Go on, Claire," said Ms. Bunting.

"I don't wanna," whimpered Claire, but she went anyway.

For a moment, she just stood on the stage in her sailor outfit. I thought maybe she had succumbed to stage fright, but at last she whispered, "*I'm Popeye the sailor man.*"

"Louder!" I called to her.

Claire raised her voice. She finished the song and danced the hornpipe. She looked totally uninspired. But then she began the song again, this time with the gestures. When she made her first face, the audience laughed. Claire hammed it up. The audience laughed harder. Claire hammed it up even more. We had a comedienne on our hands.

Kristy flashed me the thumbs-up sign and I grinned.

After Claire came a girl who played the piano (sort of), and a girl who tried to twirl a baton but kept dropping it. Then Karen Brewer, looking beautiful, ran onstage wearing the exact same outfit she had worn when she was the flower girl in her father's wedding. What, I wondered, was Karen going to do? Sing a love song or something? No. She opened her mouth and let loose with, "The wheels on the bus go round and round." She sang fifteen verses, most of which she must have made up herself, possibly right there on the stage. Verses like, "The people on the bus are tired and hot . . ." or "The dog in his carrier says, 'Let me out!' . . ." The judges began to look at their watches.

Kristy and I looked at each other and

shrugged. We weren't sure how Karen had done.

Two more girls performed, one of whom, a ballerina, was pretty good. Then Sabrina Bouvier made her entrance. I am not kidding — she was wearing a long black evening gown and white gloves that went up over her elbows. Her hair was piled onto her head like Ms. Bunting's. She sang some song I'd never heard of called "Moon River."

She was awful.

But she smiled a lot and the judges seemed to like her.

At long last it was Margo's turn. She padded onto the stage, banana in hand, sat down, and peeled the banana with her feet.

I heard snickering in the audience. It was the triplets.

Margo professionally ignored them. She launched into "This Is the House That Jack Built." Since the stanzas of the poem get longer and longer, her performance went on for quite some time. In all honesty, I'm not sure that everyone understood just what she was doing with the banana, but they appreciated all her memorizing. Margo didn't miss a beat or a word. She left the stage with applause ringing in her ears.

(Another thumbs-up from Kristy.)

All you have to know about the rest of the talent show is that there were four more contestants including Charlotte, and none of them was much good — *especially* not Charlotte, who completely forgot this passage from *Charlie and the Chocolate Factory* which she'd tried to memorize. She ran off the stage in tears. In fact, she refused to go on the stage again at all, and began crying so hard that Claudia had to go into the auditorium and find her parents so they could take her home.

Claudia looked crushed but decided to stay around to see what happened.

"Bummer," I said.

"Yeah," agreed Claudia. "Well, now I'll just have to root for Claire and Margo and Karen and Myriah. No playing favorites."

The beauty parade came next, and I'm ashamed to say that by this time, the contestants were growing good and wary of each other. It was every little miss for herself. I heard Margo tell Claire to break a leg (and she really meant it), and I heard Claire reply, "I hope you fall off the stage."

But nobody fell off the stage.

The contestants, wearing their third outfits, filed across the stage in age order. I was beginning to feel like a real stage mother.

"Smile," I reminded each Pike girl as they were about to walk onto the stage.

They smiled like Cheshire cats.

It was time for the questions. My heart began to beat faster. I'd been uncertain about the talent show because I didn't know how the audience would react to the girls — but at least I'd known what the girls were going to do. The questions were a different story. Would Claire talk about Cabbage Patch dolls and fire extinguishers? Would Margo be asked to explain what she meant by global peace?

"I'm more nervous about this than anything else," I said to Mary Anne, and she nodded in agreement, frowning worriedly.

The youngest little miss was called onto the stage, and Mrs. Peabody regarded her thoughtfully. "What," she began, "do you like best about Stoneybrook?"

Whoa! What was that? A trick question?

The little girl frowned. "The ice-cream store," she replied.

The audience laughed gently.

I knew the kid had blown it.

The next girl didn't do much better.

Myriah's turn. She walked confidently onto the stage.

"If you could change one thing about this world, what would it be?" Mrs. Peabody asked her.

"It would be wars," Myriah replied seriously. "I would stop them. I would say to the people who were making the wars, 'Now you stop that. You settle this problem yourselves like grown-ups. Our children want peace.' That's what I'd change."

The audience applauded solemnly.

"Good job!" I whispered to Mary Anne. "Myriah was great. The audience loves her. I think she's really got a chance at the crown!"

"You do?" Mary Anne replied hopefully.

"Definitely. She's the most talented contestant here — you heard the audience cheering — and she's doing great in everything else."

"Hey, Dawn," Mary Anne replied. "It's Claire's turn."

I whirled around.

Ms. Bunting had just prodded Claire onto the stage. Claire walked to Mrs. Peabody.

"Claire," said the judge, "what do you hope for most of all?"

I held my breath.

"Santa Claus," whispered Claire, looking terrified. "I hope he's real."

The audience laughed. I groaned.

"Too bad," Mary Anne said. "She got nervous. Just like Charlotte. I don't blame her."

"Thanks," I said.

Karen Brewer's question was the one about the house on fire.

"She's prepared," I heard Kristy mutter, but she leaned around me and watched Karen anxiously.

You could almost see the wheels turning in Karen's head. She wanted to say the "right" thing—what Kristy had told her to say—but she simply couldn't bear to be dishonest. She answered, "I'd rescue Moosie my stuffed cat, and Tickly my blanket, and as many toys as I could carry. Oh, could I rescue a fourth thing? If I could, it would be my brother Andrew. Or maybe my pen that writes in three colors."

Another blown answer. Karen could kiss the crown good-bye.

It was too bad that Sabrina Bouvier went on before Margo because she used up the "global peace" answer in response to her question. So when Margo was asked what she would most wish to happen in the year 2010, she froze. She didn't want to look like a copycat, and I guess she couldn't think of anything else that was *nice*. After about thirty seconds of dead silence, Mrs. Peabody gently directed her off the stage. The audience clapped politely.

I put my head in my hands. Neither Claire nor Margo was going to win.

"Hey," said Claudia, "don't feel too bad. At least your contestants stuck it out."

"I wanted *one* of them to win *something*, though. I wanted to prove how good I could be with kids."

"You did!?" exclaimed Kristy. "So did I. I guess we all did. Maybe we learned something, though. Even the best baby-sitter can't *change* a kid."

"Yeah," agreed Mary Anne. "And I'd rather have a kid like any one of ours than like Sabrina Bouvier."

We agreed wholeheartedly with that. Then we fell silent. The contestants were filing onto the stage once again. It was time for the winners to be announced.

"Myriah's going to win!" Kristy exclaimed softly. "I just know it!"

Mary Anne looked a little faint, so we gathered around her with support. None of us felt jealous anymore — not of each other, anyway. We just wanted one of our kids to win, whoever it was. I'd be as happy with Myriah as with Margo or Claire.

"The second runner-up," cried the announcer, "is Little Miss Lisa Shermer, our ballerina!"

The audience cheered as Lisa stepped out of the line and crossed the stage to stand by Mrs. Peabody.

"The first runner-up is . . . Little Miss Myriah Perkins!"

I heard two sounds just then. A shriek of joy from Myriah, who, I'm sure, was thinking of Toy City, and a cry of anguish from Mary Anne.

"Why isn't she the *grand* winner?" she wailed.

But everyone quieted down as the announcer went on, "And now, folks, the moment you've been waiting for." (Someone handed Mrs. Peabody a small crown and a bouquet of roses.) "I am happy to announce that our very own Little Miss Stoneybrook is . . . Sabrina Bouvier!"

The audience burst into applause, music began to play, and Sabrina was crowned. Photographers took her picture.

Mrs. Bouvier cried.

It was really disgusting.

My friends and I held a vehement, tortured conversation.

"Sabrina! How *could* they?!" exclaimed Kristy. "Myriah should have won."

"Told you," said Claudia knowingly. "Sabrina's a pageant-head. That's how these things work."

Our conversation came to an abrupt end as the contestants straggled backstage. As you can imagine, most of them were not very happy. In fact, Margo and Karen were in tears. They were both crying so hard they couldn't speak. When Margo dried her eyes and nose on the hem of her velvet dress, I didn't scold her. I just knelt down, took her in my arms and held her, letting her cry for as long as she needed to.

Nearby, Kristy was doing the same with Karen.

After a long time, Margo gulped and sniffled and said, "I tried my hardest, Dawn, honest."

"I know you did."

"And we're proud of you," added a voice.

Margo and I looked up. There were Mr. and Mrs. Pike and Mallory.

"Why are you proud of me?" asked Margo.

I glanced at Mallory, who gave me a look that said, "See what beauty pageants can cause?"

I shrugged. What else could I do? Claire and Margo had *wanted* to be in the pageant. It was their idea. This wasn't like Charlotte, who'd had mixed feelings about being in it.

"We're proud of you, honey," said Mr. Pike, leaning over and cupping Margo's chin in his hands, "because you were very, very brave to go out there on that stage in front of so many people. That took real courage. And you rehearsed hard. Both you and Claire did. We're proud of you for that, too."

I turned away. I had no idea Margo would take losing so hard, but I guess I should have known.

I left her with her parents and looked around for Claire. I saw her talking to Myriah, Mary Anne, and Mr. and Mrs. Perkins. Claire didn't look upset at all. I guess different kids react different ways to the same experiences. Karen was still crying against Kristy's shoulder.

I joined Claire and Mary Anne and the Perkinses. I reached them just in time to hear Mary Anne say (again), "Myriah should have won the grand prize."

"But then I wouldn't have won the toys!" exclaimed Myriah, looking amazed.

Something occurred to me then. It was all about the unfairness of the pageant. Mary Anne was absolutely right. Myriah really should have won — if this pageant was honestly based on people's talents and character. But it wasn't. I was glad that because Myriah had been given such a terrific prize, she wasn't disappointed about not winning the grand prize. But I was sorry that she had to settle (even happily) for second best.

Mallory wandered over to us then, followed by Jessi, who I guess had been in the audience.

"Don't say it," I said to them. "I know. We all should have listened to you guys on the day the newspaper article came out."

"Well . . ." said Mal, and I could tell that she and Jessi were just dying to gloat.

"I only want to say one thing," Jessi spoke up. "And I promise it isn't 'I told you so.' I want to say that now maybe it's clear how silly pageants are. I mean, look who won . . . and look who *should* have won."

"I know, I know, I know," I said testily. "I was thinking the same thing. I don't know what this pageant judged, but it sure wasn't talent and character."

"It was fake personality," Mallory pronounced.

I had to agree with her.

"Dawn?" said Claire. "Can I be in the pageant again next year?"

I nearly passed out. It was time to join the rest of the Pikes — quick! — and get home.

# CHAPTER 15

It took everyone — especially Charlotte — quite a while to get over the pageant. After all, Charlotte was the one who had run away in tears and had to be taken home.

Us baby-sitters discussed the pageant endlessly. The six of us sat around in Claudia's room most of Sunday afternoon. After we talked about how Mal and Jessi had been right, and the pageant wasn't fair and all that, Claudia (who looked a little teary-eyed) said, "I did a terrible thing."

"*What?*" asked the rest of us.

"I *forced* Charlotte into the pageant. I've apologized four times to her and her parents and they're being really nice about it, but I still feel awful."

"Well, you didn't actually *force* her into the pageant," Mary Anne pointed out. "You didn't pick her up and carry her kicking and screaming onto the stage."

"No," agreed Claudia, "but I did have to talk her into it."

"Well, I kind of did the same thing with Myriah," Mary Anne replied.

"And I kind of did the same thing with Karen," added Kristy. "They both *wanted* to be in the pageant, but we brought the subject up, hoping that that would happen. . . . And all so we could prove what good sitters we are. Pretty dumb. We *know* we're good sitters or we wouldn't have this great club!"

The rest of us laughed. But we couldn't forget the pageant. Not easily.

First an article about it and a picture of Sabrina, Myriah, and Lisa appeared in the paper. Then Myriah had her shopping spree at Toy City, and an article about *that* appeared in the paper. Then the town gave Sabrina a parade. (I don't know anyone who went to it, but another article appeared in the paper.)

I was sitting at home one evening, reading the latest article, when the phone rang. "I'll get it!" I called to Mom. I was waiting for Mary Anne to call me when she got home from the movies.

"Hello?" I said.

The voice on the other end wasn't Mary Anne's. It was Jeff's!

"Hi!" I cried. He and Dad had called twice before and spoken to Mom, but I'd been out both times. "How are you?"

"Good," replied Jeff. "Great. How are you?"

"I'm fine. Tell me what's going on. How's Dad? How's California?"

"Dad's fine, but California may not be. We had a little earthquake this afternoon."

"Whoa. Too bad. But tell me about yourself. How are you really?"

"I'm really fine. I like school. I haven't been in a single fight."

"Do you like the housekeeper Dad found?"

"Sure. She's all right. Sometimes she's kind of strict, but she's a good cook. Guess what. Most of my old friends are in my class at school. And they're all on the soccer team, so I might join the soccer team."

"And how about you and Dad? How are you getting along?"

"The bachelor life?" teased Jeff. "It's great. We went to a football game. And Dad helps me with my math." (Two things Mom and I had never done with my brother.) "Mostly I just like being someplace where everything is familiar. I feel like I was never in Stoneybrook. Kind of like it was just a weird, bad dream."

"Thanks a lot!" I exclaimed.

"Oh, you know what I mean."

"Lucky for you."

"Hey, Dawn? Dad wants to say hi. And then I want to talk to Mom, okay?"

"Okay. . . . Hi, Dad!"

"Hi, Sunshine." (Sunshine was Dad's baby name for me. If any of my friends ever heard about it . . . well, I don't even want to *think* what they'd say.) "How's my girl?"

"Fine. I miss you. So does Mom." (I wasn't sure she did, but it couldn't hurt to say so.)

I talked to Dad for a few minutes, then he talked to Mom, then Mom talked to Jeff, and finally Jeff asked to talk to me again.

"Dawn?" he said. "I just want to tell you something. Um, I miss you."

"I miss you, too," I replied, choking on the words.

" 'Bye, Dawn."

" 'Bye, Jeff."

We hung up.

"Want to make some popcorn, honey?" asked Mom, seeing my teary eyes.

"Sure," I answered.

When it was ready, we sat on the living room couch with the bowl between us.

"You know what?" I said to Mom. "That was the old Jeff on the phone. The Jeff I knew before we left California. He does seem happier there."

"He *is* happier," Mom agreed. "Letting him go may have been the toughest thing we ever did, but it was the right thing."

"I know," I said, and sighed.

"I don't want to lecture," said Mom.

"But?" I prompted her, and we laughed.

"But," she went on, "most of the best things in life *are* tough — tough to work out, or tough to achieve. If they weren't, we wouldn't appreciate them so much."

"Yeah," I agreed slowly.

The phone rang again then. "Oh, that's Mary Anne!" I said. "I'll be right back. I won't stay on long." I dashed into the kitchen, picked up the phone, and said, "Hi, Mary Anne! . . . Oh, sorry. . . . Claire?"

It was Claire Pike. She'd never called me before.

"Guess what?" she cried. "There's going to be a Beautiful Child contest at Bellair's Department Store. The winner will get to model clothes in a big fashion show at the store. Mom said I could enter — if you'll help me. Will you? Will you, Dawn?"

Oh, *no!* I thought.

"Dawn?"

"I'm here."

"The winner gets a camera, too. And a supply of Turtlewax, whatever that is."

I paused. At last I said, "Okay, Claire. Tell me what we have to do."

Here we go again!

## About the Author

ANN M. MARTIN did *a lot* of baby-sitting when she was growing up in Princeton, New Jersey. Now her favorite baby-sitting charge is her cat, Mouse, who lives with her in her Manhattan apartment.

Ann Martin's Apple Paperbacks are *Bummer Summer, Inside Out, Stage Fright, Me and Katie (the Pest),* and all the other books in the Baby-sitters Club series.

She is a former editor of books for children, and was graduated from Smith College. She likes ice cream, the beach, and *I Love Lucy*; and she hates to cook.

Look for #16

## JESSI'S SECRET LANGUAGE

"Hey, Jessi, the Barretts are here, too," Mallory whispered, as Haley, Matt, and I stepped inside. "They're friends from down the street. Buddy is eight and Suzi is five." She turned to Haley and Matt, said hello, and waved at the same time. She knew that much about signing from me. I loved her for remembering to do it. That's one of the reasons she's my new best friend.

"Well," said Mallory, "everyone's playing in the backyard."

We walked through the Pikes' house, waving to Mrs. Pike on the way, and stepped into the yard. It looked like a school playground.

The Pikes and the Barretts all stopped what they were doing and ran to us.

The introductions began.

The signings began.

The explaining began.

The staring began.

And Haley began to look angry again.

I glanced at Mallory. "Ick-en-spick," she whispered. And with that, a wonderful idea came to me. Mallory and I love to read, and not long ago we'd both read a really terrific book (even if it was a little old-fashioned) called *The Secret Language*, by Ursula Nordstrom. These two friends make up a secret language, and "ick-en-spick" is a word they use when something is silly or unnecessary.

"You know," I said to the kids, "maybe Matt can't hear or talk, but he knows a *secret language*. He can talk with his *hands*. He can say anything he wants and never make a sound."

"Really?" asked Margo (who's seven) in a hushed voice.

Mallory smiled at me knowingly. "Think how useful that would be," she said to her brothers and sisters, "if, like, Mom and Dad punished you and said, 'No talking for half an hour.' You could talk and they'd never know it."

"Yeah," said Nicky slowly. "Awesome."

"How do you do it?" asked Vanessa. "What's the secret language?"

## Here's some news about other books in The Baby-sitters Club series by Ann M. Martin

### #1   Kristy's Great idea

Kristy thinks the Baby-sitters Club is a great idea. She and her friends Claudia, Stacey, and Mary Anne all love taking care of kids. But nobody counted on crank calls, wild pets, and uncontrollable two-year-olds! Having a Baby-sitters Club isn't easy, but Kristy and her friends won't give up till they get it right!

### #2   Claudia and the Phantom Phone Calls

Claudia has been getting some mysterious phone calls when she's out baby-sitting. Could they be from the Phantom Jewel Thief who's operating in the area? Claudia has always liked *reading* mysteries, but she doesn't like it when they *happen* to her!

### #3   The Truth About Stacey

The truth about Stacey is her parents want to find a miracle cure for her diabetes. They're making Stacey's life so hard! The other Baby-sitters are busy fighting the Baby-sitters Agency. How can they help Stacey and save the club, too?

## #4  *Mary Anne Saves the Day*

Mary Anne's never been a leader of the Baby-sitters Club. Now there's a big fight among the four friends. It's bad enough when Mary Anne has to eat at the lunch table all alone. But when she has to baby-sit a sick child with no help from her friends — it's time to take charge!

## #5  *Dawn and the Impossible Three*

Poor Dawn! It's not easy being the newest member of the Baby-sitters Club. She's got three impossible kids to take care of. And Kristy thinks things were better *without* Dawn around. It'll take a lot of work to make things run smoothly again, but Dawn's up to the challenge!

## #6  *Kristy's Big Day*

It's a big day for Kristy, all right — she's a bridesmaid in her mother's wedding! And if that's not enough, she and the other Baby-sitters Club members have *fourteen* wedding-guest kids to take care of. Only the Baby-sitters Club could cope with this one!

## #7 Claudia and Mean Janine

This summer the Baby-sitters Club is starting a play group in the neighborhood. Claudia can't wait for it to begin — it'll give her some time away from her mean big sister. But then her grandmother has a stroke . . . and the whole summer changes.

## #8 Boy-Crazy Stacey

Who needs baby-sitting when there are boys around? Stacey and Mary Anne are mother's helpers at the Jersey shore, and Stacey's mind is on hunky lifeguard Scott. Mary Anne's doing the work of two baby-sitters . . . but how can she tell Stacey that Scott's too old, without breaking Stacey's heart?

## #9 The Ghost at Dawn's House

Creaking stairs, noises behind the wall, a secret passage — there must be a ghost at Dawn's house! The Baby-sitters find themselves and one of their charges wrapped up in a mystery. Will they be able to solve it?

## #10  *Logan Likes Mary Anne!*

Quiet, shy Mary Anne has been growing up lately . . . and the Baby-sitters aren't the only ones who've noticed. Logan Bruno likes Mary Anne! He has a dreamy southern accent, he's awfully cute — and he wants to join the Baby-sitters Club. Life in the club has never been this complicated — or this fun!

## #11  *Kristy and the Snobs*

The kids in Kristy's new neighborhood aren't very friendly. In fact they're . . . well, snobs. They laugh at everything — even Kristy's poor old collie, Louie. Kristy's fighting mad. But if anyone can beat a Snob attack, it's the Baby-sitters club. And that's just what they're going to do!

## #12  *Claudia and the New Girl*

Claudia really likes Ashley, the new girl at school. Ashley's the only one who takes Claudia seriously. Soon, Claudia's spending so much time with Ashley that she doesn't have time for baby-sitting — or her old friends. And they don't like it one bit!

## #13   Good-bye Stacey, Good-bye

There are lots of tears when the Baby-sitters hear the news: Stacey and her family are moving back to New York. The club members can't think of a special enough way to send Stacey off. They want to give her much more than a party. But how do you say good-bye to your best friend?

## #14   Hello, Mallory

Mallory Pike has always been good at baby-sitting her younger brothers and sisters. But is she good enough to join the Baby-sitters Club? The club members go overboard giving Mallory baby-sitting tests. Mallory's getting pretty fed up. . . . Maybe she'll just start a baby-sitting business of her own!

## #16   Jessi's Secret Language

Jessi had a hard time fitting in to Stoneybrook. But things got a lot better once she became a member of the Baby-sitters Club! Now Jessi has her biggest challenge yet — baby-sitting for a deaf boy. And in order to communicate with him, Jessi must learn his secret language.

# THE BABY-SITTERS CLUB®

## by Ann M. Martin

*More titles...* ➤

$2.95
$2.95
$3.25
$3.25
$3.25
$3.25
$2.95
$3.25
$3.25
$2.95
$3.25
$3.25
$3.25
$3.25
$3.25
$3.25
$3.25
$3.25
$3.25
$3.25
$3.25
$3.50
$3.50
$3.50
$3.50
$3.50
$3.50
$3.50

quest
al #2
#3
#4

form.
MO 65102

g $_____
order - no

City_____ State/Zip _____
Please allow four to six weeks for delivery. Offer good in the U.S. only. Sorry, mail orders are not
ices subject to change.

BSC991

A0001500003239